THE HARDLINERS

Edmund Crispin in the *Sunday Times* has praised
William Haggard's "gift for making the reader feel
that he has been taken by the hand, led behind the
scenes, and shown where real power lies." With
Charles Russell back in the arena, moving in the
harsh world that lies beneath the high-flown language of diplomacy, the power game takes on a new
and exciting ambience.

Also by William Haggard

A COOL DAY FOR KILLING
THE DOUBTFUL DISCIPLE

and published by Corgi Books

WILLIAM HAGGARD

THE HARDLINERS

CORGI BOOKS
A DIVISION OF TRANSWORLD PUBLISHERS LTD
A NATIONAL GENERAL COMPANY

THE HARDLINERS

A CORGI BOOK 0 552 08988 5

Originally published in Great Britain
by Cassell & Co. Ltd.

PRINTING HISTORY
Cassell edition published 1970
Corgi edition published 1972

Corgi Books are published by Transworld Publishers Ltd.,
Cavendish House, 57–59 Uxbridge Road, Ealing, London W.5.
Made and printed in Great Britain by
Hazell Watson & Viney Ltd., Aylesbury, Bucks

THE HARDLINERS

CHAPTER ONE

Colonel Charles Russell, lately of the Security Executive and now its grey eminence, was dining with Sir Fenton Omerod who'd been known before his knighthood by the much less patrician name of William. The Fenton had been his mother's name but also he'd been christened with it, and he'd elected for Fenton as more impressive. He was that sort of man. Russell had met and didn't admire him, but he was beholden to his daughter and he always paid his debts. She had a column in a Sunday newspaper, straight down the middle well-written comment, which meant that all the clever ones, those on the Right as well as the Left, despised it as part of the Sunday pulp. But that didn't stop it selling the paper; indeed it was one of its major features, read by as many men as women. Julia Hartley was well known and better paid.

More important, she'd been one of Charles Russell's sources. Not of information as such. Not, for instance, that the mistress of a senior Minister was the American wife of the chairman of an aircraft firm, nor even that the Honourable Member for West Witherspoon took his orders direct from a foreign embassy. These facts Russell knew: they'd been part of his daily diet. What Julia had told him had been simply who else knew, or rather who knew and might also use it. It was safe to assume that the Press would *know*, but what was its evidence, what was the *smell*? What paper had motive to pull out the carpet, what board was prepared for a full-dress suit for libel? In all this and much else Julia had been Charles Russell's ears, and now he was paying a part of his obligation. She had asked him to talk to her father, to deflate him if he could do so. Of course as gently as possible. He seemed to think that these memoirs of his were going to be an immense success, making him the Man of the Year instead of just another retired ambassador. Julia, a journalist, feared they'd fall stillborn from the Maidenhair Press.

He was saying to Russell importantly: 'I'd like your opinion on this Beaujolais. Juliénas, you know, the table wine of the Lyonnais. I get it from my club's wine merchants.'

Charles Russell sipped. 'Very nice,' he said politely and indeed the wine was drinkable. But it wasn't worth serious comment. Charles Russell loved wine but detested wineman-ship. If this perfectly ordinary bottle had been his he'd have put it on the table without a word, not praising (it wasn't worth it) and certainly not apologizing. 'So you're an author now,' he said. 'When does the book come out?'

'Not till the autumn. It takes at least nine months to get a book out.'

'It sounds a long time.'

'It's the printing unions—they're far too powerful.'

Charles Russell sighed softly, not at the view which very possibly was right, but it struck him as merely stupid to state it, more precisely to state it as Omerod did, with more than a hint of resentment, pontifically. . . . The country is going to pot, you know. Not a doubt of it, my dear fellow.

Russell ate on deliberately, half-listening to Sir Fenton. He was good at half-listening, deceptively good as many men had discovered. He knew Omerod's history, and if pressed for a single word for his feelings would simply have said he was sorry. Omerod had gone close to the top but Sir Fenton hadn't made it. And every human value he'd had had gone into that career of his, considerable intelligence and some sympathy before he'd burnt it out. He'd set up his model young and he'd aped it slavishly, the perfect, the twenty-two-carat British diplomat. And then the fashion had suddenly changed and Sir Albert Bull was Permanent Under-Secretary. That Albert Bull! Charles Russell hid a smile, for he knew what Fenton Omerod thought about Bull. Both men had come from quite modest backgrounds but Bull had never concealed it nor bothered to try. So now he was P.U.S. and Sir Fenton wasn't; he'd been Ambassador to a state in central Europe and then the chop. Russell didn't know whether to smile or pity. Mostly his pity came out top.

Sir Fenton was talking on about his book, distressingly displaying all the symptoms of first authorship. Russell glanced at Julia : Julia nodded.

'I wish you every success, I do indeed. But you know what a bitch the goddess is.'

Omerod looked up sharply, his lips forming. 'What do you mean?' but training won. Instead he asked coolly: 'You are trying to convey something?'

Charles Russell didn't answer him—there wasn't an answer a guest could make. 'I believe it's being published by the Maidenhair Press.'

'And you're thinking I might have done better? I don't agree. Bigger publishers have more money no doubt, but Vane has the literary reputation.'

Russell didn't answer again. He'd once been to one of Vane's exquisite little dinner parties, where he'd been fairly well fed and cruelly bored. These hand-picked little parties had undeniably a *cachet* but they didn't attract the writers who sold.

Fenton was saying dangerously: 'You think I should have gone to Mackellars?'

'As you hinted yourself, they're very much bigger.'

'That's why I didn't go to them.'

'I've a glimmering of your motives but if I ever wrote a book myself I'd be vulgar enough to want it to sell.'

Fenton said with astonishing vehemence: 'This one will sell, by God it will.'

'Father—' Julia Hartley said.

'I've been talking about my book too much.' He looked at his daughter. 'Talking before a professional too.' He contrived it to mean anything. 'I suggest that we change the subject.' He looked at Charles Russell. 'And how are you finding retirement?'

'Much as I'd hoped—the day isn't long enough.'

'You're a very fortunate man indeed.'

'Not fortunate, quite. I thought ahead.'

'Is that a reproof?'

'No, call it a grace.'

They had coffee in the library, a fine if over-furnished room, paid for as was the house itself by Agnes's money, Fenton Omerod's dead wife. She'd left him that, Charles Russell remembered, since leaving it to her latest lover would have struck her as very improper indeed. So she'd left him her money but nothing else, and certainly no kind memories. Not that Charles Russell blamed her. She'd been married for her money and been perfectly aware of it, but to the heiress of a successful builder William Omerod as he'd then called himself had seemed a very good match in every way. Her mother had approved of him though her father had barely concealed his contempt, this elegant young sprig with the upper crust manners he'd painfully copied, the Foreign Office airs and graces. The shrewd business man had seen through him at once but Agnes hadn't till much too late. The wife of a diplomatist—the prospect had been dazzling.

Inevitably he had let her down. For it hadn't been Paris, New York or Rome, it had been drear Asian states and a spell in Sweden, Consul General of this, Head of Chancery of that. She'd known he'd get his knighthood since in the Foreign Office they were two a penny, the meanest state feeling insulted if Her Majesty's representative there wasn't loaded with cut-price honours. Other men in Whitehall knew their total lack of value and so had Agnes Omerod, but it wouldn't be disagreeable to be a Lady when the card came up, and it probably would—the odds were on it. They were, that is, if he didn't divorce her, but he'd never do that, he hadn't a penny. So she'd given him a daughter and called it a day, horning him quite shamelessly. Russell couldn't have said he approved but nor did he judge. What a stuffed shirt the man was, what a walking dummy! And poor Agnes had died before the knighthood, the embassy in middle Europe. She probably wouldn't have gone with him but at least she'd be Lady Omerod. She never had for she'd died in a car crash. Charles Russell frowned for he hadn't disliked her. He thought she'd had a shabby deal.

Omerod was offering brandy now, making a senseless fuss again, and again it was neither good nor bad. He drank two glasses to Russell's one and at half past ten began to nod. He was a man who needed a great deal of sleep.

'If you'll excuse me I'll turn in. I've been working rather hard, you know. You have everything you want?'

'Everything, thank you.'

'I've had Vichy put in your room, of course.'

'How very kind.'

'Not at all. Good night.'

His daughter watched him walk out of the room with an expression which Russell noticed but couldn't read. She was an intelligent woman so it was inconceivable she admired him, but the look had been more than tolerant, even fierce. Affection? Hardly. A good daughter's protective instinct? Perhaps. Or perhaps simply that rarest of contemporary virtues, an old-fashioned sense of obligation.

But she was smiling at Russell, talking again. 'Thank you for trying anyway, Charles.'

'I'm afraid it didn't go down very well.'

'I brought you here on a real fool's errand. He's crazy about that book of his.'

'I've seen it before, a man writes a book—'

'But there's more to it than that, I think.' She hesitated but finally said it. She and Charles Russell were very old friends. 'I know people think he's stupid but he's not. Not in that way, at least. He's too experienced.'

'But just another Ambassador's memoirs—'

'*If that's all they are.*'

He sat up sharply. 'Meaning?'

'Charles, I'm a journalist. I hear things. And I'll lay you another brandy you still hear too.'

'The bet goes down, you lose the brandy.' Charles Russell rose and helped himself. 'All right, so I still hear things.'

'And you know where his last post was?'

'Yes, of course.'

'And you know perfectly well what's happened there.'

'But two months after your father left.'

She said reflectively : 'It's a bore to go on saying that I'm writing for a newspaper, but it does condition the way you think. I don't believe one of the super powers acts in the way that that one did simply for ideological reasons. There are people maybe who think like that but I don't believe they hold the levers.'

'I know they don't. Go on.'

'Sending tanks into an allied country, annoying the Americans, endangering any *détente* with them—'

'We haven't heard the whole story yet and probably we

never shall.'

'Suppose father knew it.'

'How the hell could he know it?' Russell was taken aback and showed it.

'He *was* a diplomatist.'

'He was Her Majesty's Ambassador.'

'And outside Her Majesty's sphere of influence?'

'Very much out,' Charles Russell said dryly.

'But he might have been a go-between.'

'That's stretching it, purest guessing.'

'Agreed that I've nothing to go on, but it isn't what he says, it's what he doesn't. And he does seem amazingly confident.'

'If that book is an inch within what you suggest then it's going to sell a million. Rejoice.'

'But I don't rejoice, I'm scared to death.'

'Of what the Foreign Office might say or do?'

She said something dismissive about the Office.

'Then of what?'

'Charles, you worked in that world for twenty years, you know it isn't a nursery.'

He considered it carefully. 'I take the point. If there *is* a story it won't be a pretty one. There'd be people who'd like to see it suppressed.'

'Powerful people?'

'Powerful enough.'

'Can you help him, Charles?'

'Not as things stand. It isn't because I'm retired, I don't say that. They still come to me for advice if you call it that, and I could put the machine in gear if I chose. But not on what you're telling me, not on a single guess at some secret.'

'I realize that and I wasn't asking. But you'll keep a fatherly eye on it?'

'I've always wished I'd had a daughter.'

They went upstairs and Charles Russell undressed. He noticed the bottle of Vichy and smiled. In Omerod's house it would have to be Vichy. The heat was too high and he turned it down. Since the English had taken to central heating they'd been absurdly overdoing it. He lay down on the bed with a last cigar, for he seldom slept much before one o'clock. This was still the best moment of any day, in the past much too often the only one tolerable, the minutes before sleep came, the knowledge it would. Of course one had to train oneself, to put out the light and deal sensibly with that last cigar. No burning the bed up, no sickening stench when the dawn crept in coldly. Meanwhile this was bliss or such bliss as earth offered. He watched the pale smoke curl upwards slowly.

So he'd told Fenton Omerod he was happy in retirement. That had been wholly true for he'd long considered it. He had kept on his London flat since it suited him well, an easy drive to any of three golf courses, and when he felt like real country he had a rod on a Hampshire river and a room in the house which went with it. Charles Russell, born a countryman, would have been happy enough in the country, but only given established roots, land and the need to care for it. By now he was a townsman and unashamed. This grand Surrey villa of Fenton Omerod's was precisely what he would never have chosen. It was imposing, even opulent, but bore less relation to where it stood than Charles Russell's maisonette to its London street. It was a sham, a denial, something for the Sir Fentons, not for Russell. He much preferred his Italian hideout which he'd bought for a song twenty years ago.

Yes, his days were full, he was well content, and it was also true what he'd said to Julia. The Executive did still come to him, bringing him the awkward ones. He'd agreed and even invited it and they'd taken him at his word and more. The man who'd taken his place was shaking down, and Russell couldn't have ridden him even if he had wished to. The daily routine he had sloughed without a sigh. That, after all, was why one retired. He was never bored, was indeed contented. He'd spoken the truth then, but not quite all of it. For it wasn't quite the same thing, it really wasn't. He did miss something and sometimes badly. Responsibility was the word for it. He'd been trained all his life to carry it and however much advice they asked, much more than he'd expected they would, it could never fulfil him as action had.

Well, that was what being sixty meant.

He was conscious that sleep was stalking him and opened

a window to throw out his butt. Then he shut it again quite silently. He sat down on the bed and considered it. A light was on downstairs, someone was moving, and whoever it was wasn't hiding his prowl. Russell looked at his watch: it was five to one.

He put on slippers and a dressing gown and walked quietly into the gallery over the hall. He'd thought the noise had come from the library but the door was shut and he couldn't see in. On the other side of the hall a door was open, light shining out from the gunroom strongly. That was what Fenton Omerod called it, a pomposity Charles Russell thought, but gunroom it was in the sense that a glass-fronted cabinet held just two weapons. They were a shotgun and a rook rifle. Fenton was moving out now with the shotgun, slipping in two cartridges, closing the breech. He held the gun at the ready and crossed the hall, checking at the library door. Then he threw it open suddenly. He put in a hand and felt for the switch and the lights came on as he snapped it down. Fenton Omerod went in deliberately. Russell heard him call out:

'Who's there?'

Not surprisingly, nobody answered. Charles Russell stood still and worried quietly, not that Fenton Omerod would be running into a danger but that the fool would do some extravagant harm to whoever might be the intruder. Russell had excellent eyesight still and in the light from the open gunroom door he'd noticed Omerod's cartridges. One had been normal, the other hadn't: it had protruded at the business end. Ball—unmistakable. Fired from the choke it was messily lethal. And Charles Russell knew well how Sir Fenton would think. There were some fine things in this pretentious house but a fence wouldn't think so nor deal in them gladly. It wasn't the sort of establishment to attract a major gang from London—no furs, little jewellery. So the intruder would be the local bad man or maybe some boy on the run from Borstal, looking for what he could find and hope to flog.

Which wouldn't affect Sir Fenton in any way. . . . Damn it, the house is mine, my *property*. Some criminal breaks in. . . . What did you expect me to do, watch him rob me? Yes,

I know there are rules about self-defence, but they're degenerate nonsense, eyewash for judges who don't know their duty.

Sir Fenton would shoot at sight and be pleased to do so. Thereafter he'd lie his head off about some attack on him which hadn't happened. His voice came up to Russell again.

'Who's there? God damn you—answer.'

There was the noise of a sudden movement, then a sickening unmistakable sound, a blow on an unprotected head. Russell began to move at once, down the stairs in long strides and across the hall. The library lights were on still and he went in. The safe was open, still stuffed with papers. Omerod was on the ground before it, the unfired shotgun lying half under him.

Russell pulled out the gun and unloaded it carefully. He could sense another man's presence there but still he unloaded methodically. Men of sixty waving firearms were a foolish provocation. He felt Sir Fenton over quickly. . . . Neck not broken but breathing badly. Pulse very weak. Sir Fenton Omerod had bought it.

Charles Russell began to think hard and coolly, years of training achieving an enviable detachment. He wasn't precisely frightened but he knew he'd lost the initiative. That is, if he'd ever had it, which come to think of it he had not. . . . Search the room? It would hardly be fruitful. There were three fine windows and six fine drapes and there could well be more than a single man. Walking straight into another coshing would be something less than sensible. No, the next move was theirs, so let them make it.

Russell turned to the safe and looked in quickly. There were a good many files and a collection of legal documents, covenants, wills, conveyances, the papers of any man of means. There were also and quite illegally a quantity of Bearer Bonds ('He isn't an Authorised Depository.') Finally a pile of diaries. They were embossed with a crown and 'E.R.II.'

. . . That was really rather mean of him. He could well afford to buy his own stationery.

Russell returned from reflection unwillingly. He'd have to attend to Fenton Omerod, he couldn't just leave him lying

15

there. There was a house-phone on the impressive desk but Russell knew he would never reach it. Besides, the servants slept out. . . . Just Julia, a woman, and it seemed a sound sleeper. But he might as well get Omerod into a chair. He put his arms under Fenton Omerod's, squatting to do so, turning his back on those opulent curtains. The gesture cost him a conscious effort but he made it fatalistically. After all, he was waiting, inviting action.

He'd had Fenton half upright, his own knees straight, when the pistol came into the small of his back. He had heard no movement but that didn't surprise him. A voice said softly :

'Forty-five calibre. Blow out your liver.'

Charles Russell put Omerod carefully down.

CHAPTER TWO

Another Ambassador and this one still serving was reading an unwelcome dispatch. His Excellency was thinking with concentration and clearly, though he found the former difficult since he wasn't in good health at all. The Gestapo had seen to that and well, and though the physical scars had healed the rest remained. Now, thirty years later, he still had nightmares, bouts of recurrent and savage pain, and this week had been an extremely bad one. But if he could concentrate only with effort, he could think with exemplary clarity still; he was a hardline communist, soaked in the spring of purest doctrine, as ruthlessly brain-washed as any prefect at a Jesuit school. So this sort of thought had become a reflex, the action which followed completely conditioned.

His country was part of what anyone but a communist would have simply called an empire, and it had recently been treated as provinces always had been treated by vigorous and determined masters. His Excellency resented it but he didn't consider it wholly unjust. What were satellites for? Besides, in a way they'd asked for it, foolish men with absurd and suspect ideas. There could be no such thing as a liberalized communism, the phrase was as silly as liberal Pope. So they'd asked for it and they'd duly collected. Now a patriot's task was to ride the chill wind, for there was nothing in basic doctrine which prevented you being a patriot. Within reason of course, and subject to higher ends and wider aims. A man could love his country still but he mustn't be bourgeois nationalist.

The chill wind from the east—it was very cold. So far it had withered but it hadn't entirely blotted out, and the Ambassador thought it needn't if one behaved with a proper discretion. What His Excellency thought of as freedom, the recognition of necessity, they could still maintain if they kept their heads. No mass deportations, no openly puppet government. What the decadent West considered freedom was something quite other and unimportant.

So why had it happened and why had the tanks come? The Ambassador didn't know and he never would. He'd never been quite in the foremost rank, never in the praesidium; he was utterly loyal with a splendid record, the very stuff and essence of an Ambassador to the Court of Saint James. . . . I serve. I obey. When I must I command. When fate has one of her kinder days I may even command successfully.

A bout of pain shook him; he set his teeth. He was ageing now and his life could be demanding. One day he'd take those three pills too many; meanwhile he served on since they hadn't relieved him. He was an ageing man but still a tough one.

So some half-naked intellectuals had played with fire and burnt their fingers. He didn't blame the fire brigade since in their shoes he'd have done precisely the same, but there was a distinction between a fire brigade and an open army of occupation. It hadn't quite come to that just yet but the patience of a super power was notoriously exhaustible, and it would certainly exhaust itself if some hothead risked the system again. His Excellency re-read the decoded dispatch.

Imperative inhibit publication Omerod Memoirs.

Hm. . . . He thought he saw it. That ass Fenton Omerod had been Ambassador in his capital, which meant that he'd been in a fine position to find things out if he'd cared to do so. His Excellency was astonished that apparently he had

done just that since Omerod had always struck him as bliss-
fully stupid, the stereotype not-so-gentle Knight, the man in
gold braid with a patronizing manner, the Foreign Office
messenger boy with absurd delusions his work was important. But it seemed that he'd kept his ears open, and God
knew there'd been enough to hear. There'd been a Press
lacking discipline, the young who'd forgotten the past or
never known it, an edging towards the West and its feeble
decay.

The Ambassador frowned. The collapse of his country had
brought him much sympathy, and sympathy was always useful, though privately he despised the sympathizers. Their
moral disapproval was no substitute for practical help but
enough of it made even a super power hesitate before it
reached for the ultimate sanctions. True. But suppose that
something had really happened, something concrete and
therefore serious, more than just intangibles, a smell in the
air and a sense of false freedoms. Then there'd be men to the
east to shout it loud, 'We were justified', and the world
would listen. That wouldn't be good for his country, no indeed. One wasn't a bourgeois nationalist because one didn't
much fancy blood in the streets. His Excellency had read his
dispatch, and what had been a hunch at first hardened
sharply into near certainty. Something *had* happened and
something had leaked, and these were his clear instructions,
his orders.

He switched on the intercom and spoke into it briefly. Find
Major Josef Satra and find him quickly. Send him up to the
private office at once.

When Satra came in he gave him the message, watching
him read it, watching him think. He wasn't entirely happy
with Satra and had felt it his duty to report confidentially
that the Major had been in the West too long. He had done
so with some reluctance since he had little specific against his
Attaché. He was a good party man still and basically reli-
able; he wasn't an intellectual, he was as hard as a nail, a
soldier, a man. It would be criminal to throw him on the
scrap heap which his recall could mean, so the Ambassador
had a job for him. It wasn't at all an Attaché's line but the
Ambassador thought the distinction trifling. Moreover he

wasn't quite sure of his other staff; he couldn't be wholly sure since the tragedy. One man would look one way and one another. All had their careers at stake, especially the man he'd have normally used. But at least you could be sure of Satra, he'd think first of his simple duty and then he'd do it. When you could firmly report again—Satra had redeemed himself. That wouldn't be distasteful since His Excellency hated waste, he hated to see a good man broken. He looked at Josef Satra again as he sat reading the message silently. He wasn't a very intelligent man, perhaps he was even a trifle stolid, but he was very well worth the saving still. He sat in his chair bolt upright, virile and taut. The Ambassador said quietly:

'What do you make of it?'

'Nothing at all since you choose to ask me. It seems an inexplicable fuss about another British diplomat's memoirs.'

'A hundred thousand words of gossip?'

'What else could it be from a man like Omerod?'

'But you know where he was and when he was there. Things were happening then.'

'They certainly were. But all of that's known, the results of it too.'

'The results are known, they're most certainly known. But all of it . . .?'

'What do you mean?'

His Excellency nodded at the dispatch. 'I mean simply that those are our orders.'

He fell into silence, thinking again. When the tanks had gone in both men had wept, but they'd wept for entirely different reasons. The Ambassador had been furious that his own people could be so foolish. Could one never teach the clever boys, never educate intellectuals into the barest respect for reality? But Satra had wept in frustrated rage, using a hateful word for those others. The Ambassador didn't dissent from it since he'd spent a year in one of their prisons. By now that was almost an open credential, like a certain sort of necktie in this decadent doomed western city, but he hadn't forgotten and far less forgiven. But he never used that blistering word for he'd realized what hid behind it, futile escape. It was schoolboys calling their master pig but whatever they called him he stayed their master.

Josef Satra was asking : 'What can I do?'

'I was waiting for you to make a suggestion.' He hadn't become an Ambassador without picking up some of the simpler tricks.

'You're thinking I know Omerod's daughter?'

'I've heard that you know her rather well.'

If the reports were correct it was better than well. His Excellency didn't object in principle : on the contrary it was a most sensible contact. She was the daughter of a diplomatist, on top of that a successful journalist. But what had the friendship yielded? Nothing. There could be reasons for that —the British had tightened up of late—but it was the friendship itself which the hard old man doubted. It looked as if it were serious and that could be fatal for Josef Satra. The Ambassador drummed on the table reflectively. He was past the desire for women now, the Gestapo had diminished that need and the other prison completed their work, but he hadn't spent an unfruitful young manhood. Of course Satra needed a woman—who didn't? But being serious was different. A woman of the West—it was never on.

'You think knowing Julia Hartley could give me a line?' Josef Satra was very polite but he didn't like it.

'It's an obvious thought.'

'If I may say so, sir, too obvious. Mrs Hartley is uneasy, yes, but not about what the book contains. She's worried about what it doesn't contain. Her father's expecting great things from it, but if it's what she thinks it is it's going to disappoint him sorely.'

'So he's expecting a great success for it. Why?' The Ambassador had spoken sharply.

'I can't tell you that but we both know the man.'

'Who nevertheless might somehow have stumbled on something.'

'I suppose it's just conceivable.'

His Excellency considered it, finally nodding briefly. 'I agree Mrs Hartley cannot help us, but our orders remain to inhibit the book.'

'But how do we stop them publishing? The Maidenhair

Press is third rank at best but there are first class people who'd jump at it. They'd jump, that is, if the book blows some secret.'

'I think we must assume it does. They wouldn't have sent us instructions to bottle up gossip.'

'I'm afraid I don't see where we go from here.'

'No? But I've been in this country longer than you have, and once before as a very young man. You said that the Maidenhair Press was small beer. I don't disagree with that at all, but no publisher likes to look like a fool, not even a wet one like Peregrine Vane. And if you put out a challenging book you're going to be challenged. I don't mean with a libel suit—your editors would look after that—but it isn't quite like a newspaper. If you print in hard covers what looks like a scoop you're going to be asked to back it up. Not proof, or not proof in a court of law, but you're going to be asked where the story came from and it's no good just saying "Sir Fenton Omerod". You may not be forced to produce what you've got but you're going to be asked to declare its nature.'

'Papers, for instance? Secret papers?'

'Just possibly, but I don't think it's that.'

Josef Satra said thoughtfully : 'There was a man who kept copies of almost everything. When he used it all in those shameless books hardly anyone batted an eyelid.'

'Fenton Omerod wasn't a politician.'

'Yet if he breaks some story it's got to have some backing? According to you the book's worthless without it.'

'His diaries,' the Ambassador said. 'He's been heard to boast that he always kept diaries.'

'Which he might have cooked later to back up his story.'

'Ach! . . . His diaries mightn't be proof in a court, but I told you this wasn't a matter for lawyers.' His Excellency looked at Satra shrewdly. 'If it came to a showdown about those diaries would you dare to say publicly Omerod had cooked them?'

'Never in England. Certainly not.'

'You'd be perfectly right. He'd have your shirt.'

'Then Peregrine Vane will be holding those diaries.'

'It's possible but I don't think it follows; they'll be Omerod's cover as well as Vane's. There'll be a clause in the contract about production if necessary but I doubt if Sir Fenton has handed them over. What I do not doubt is simply this : if the diaries or something like them didn't exist then Vane wouldn't be even considering Omerod's book. And probably nobody else would either.'

'You've heard talk of these diaries and maybe more?'

'I've heard that ass doing the talking himself.'

'It's a line of a sort,' Josef Satra said.

'It's the only sort of line we have.' His Excellency looked down at his mottled old hands. The nails had never quite grown the same. 'You've been to the Omerod house, I believe. Is there a safe there?'

'I noticed one in the library.'

'Then, my friend, you are going to break it.'

Josef Satra didn't raise his voice; he was a soldier under discipline. 'Permit me with respect,' he said, 'to remind you I'm not a safebreaker.'

'You don't need to be a safebreaker.' His Excellency was as cool as ice.

'But we could send for one and use him.'

'Far too risky. If something went wrong he'd be unprotected.'

Satra said stolidly : 'Whereas if your Military Attaché is caught in the act of blowing a safe—'

'That would be common crime sure enough, and in theory they could jail you. But it's morally certain they wouldn't do that. As you say, you're an Attaché, you're properly on the books as that, and Sir Fenton's an ex-Ambassador. So foreign Attaché robs diplomat's safe. . . . Why? What was in it? *What shouldn't have been?*' His Excellency allowed a smile. 'The Foreign Office would have it hushed up, you can take my sincerest word for it.'

'But they'd have me withdrawn and I don't want that.'

'I know you don't want it. I know why too.'

There was iron in the tone now as well as ice and Josef Satra had heard it before. He made a sort of half-bow, sitting, but he asked with an open resentment :

'Is that an order?'

'Yes it is.'

'You wish me to go to some night school for criminals?'

'That will be unnecessary.' The crude sarcasm came back as an acid irony. 'It's really extremely simple, you know.'

'It doesn't sound simple to me at all.'

'I assure you it is. I did it myself many years ago and you don't need a criminal's skills in the least.'

'Please tell me,' Josef Satra said.

His Excellency the Ambassador did so.

He'd had Fenton half upright, his own knees straight, when the pistol came into the small of his back.

'Forty-five calibre. Blow out your liver.'

Russell put Omerod carefully down. The voice had been educated but had an accent he recognized. It had been central European though he couldn't place it closer than that. Nor did he need to since it hadn't been a criminal's. A criminal would have made no noise; he'd have blown the safe, scooped its contents and gone; but this man had made a deliberate noise, bringing Omerod down to open it for him. . . . A natural thing to do in alarm, to run to your safe and check what it held? Natural if there was anything in it, anything Omerod really prized. It was the first thing a man would do if he didn't think. Russell nodded approvingly. It had been the simplest of plans and therefore successful.

The pistol was still in the small of his back but he wasn't too much afraid of it. The voice had given him more than geography, some feeling for the man behind him. He might, of course, be entirely wrong, and that would cut short a deserved retirement, but Russell wasn't greatly scared that a bullet in the back was likely. He looked at the door of the open safe, seeing that it was a modern one, not the sort you could carelessly shut but leave insecure. He raised his right foot and kicked the door. There was the noise of the slam and a second of silence, then the click of the tumblers resetting themselves.

The man behind Russell began to swear. Then he said dangerously : 'And now you'll reopen it.'

'I don't know the combination.'

'Who are you then?'

'I'm a house-guest. If you press me, a reluctant one.'

23

There was a thoughtful silence. 'You're quite a bold man,' the voice said at last.

'You could say I'm no longer a young one.'

'Put your hands up. Turn round.'

'I'm a little too old to go holding my hands up. I'll keep them behind me. Right?'

'All right.'

Charles Russell turned round and stared with interest. There was a stocking mask and gloves on the hands but for Russell there was plenty more. The suit was very good indeed and Russell could guess within a street who had made it and what the work had cost. The hands were gloved and told him nothing but the shoes matched the clothes in excellence. And shoes told you more than anything else. Young men could also buy beautiful shoes but too often they let them rot on their feet. These were admirably cared for. . . . So. So a man of maybe forty who could afford good shoes and didn't shoot in the back. Mid-European accent but very good English. Held himself well and easily, head back. Maybe a soldier, maybe not.

Josef Satra for his part was looking at Russell. He was sure he had never met him and he'd never seen his photograph. This, though he didn't know it, wasn't surprising. Russell was seldom photographed and when he was they were mostly suppressed. He'd always played ball with the Press when he could and mostly they'd played it back at him. A photograph of Colonel Russell was as rare as a rose in an English December.

Satra began to speak again. 'And what were you now intending, please?'

'I really don't know—you're the man behind the gun.' Russell was rather liking this man. He was playing it without hint of humour but he'd kept his nerve and he wasn't a bully.

'Is there anyone else in this house besides you two?' Satra looked down at Fenton Omerod but he didn't move the gun an inch.

'You can't expect me to tell you that.'

'No—foolish question.' Josef Satra reflected. There'd be Julia upstairs in bed and Julia might know the combo, but she'd also know Josef Satra's voice. For that and other important reasons it simply wasn't on to wake her. He considered again and finally shrugged. 'I suggest you make me a proposition.'

'Certainly – I'd intended to. My interest here is simply a guest's.' Charles Russell looked down in turn at Sir Fenton. 'And that includes attention to whatever you've left of my one-time host.'

'That's the proper thing to do, of course.' It was a statement of fact, spoken without a shadow of irony.

'I'm a proper sort of man, you see.'

'I'd formed the same impression myself. That's why I asked for a proposition.'

'Then I'll give you three minutes, or four if you press me. Then I propose to telephone. Doctor and an ambulance. Police too. Who won't have a hope of tracing you.'

'And if I decline?'

'Then I shall have to do something foolish, force your hand. I confess it'd be reluctantly and I can't be quite sure I could make myself do it. But nor can you that I wouldn't and that's the point.'

'Four minutes of grace?'

'I said so—yes.'

'I haven't in fact a choice short of violence.' The voice wasn't resentful but simply reflective.

'And you haven't the inclination for violence?'

'How did you guess?'

'I'm good at guessing.'

Satra began a gesture which might have been a salute but checked it. 'Good night, sir,' he said.

'Good night to you.'

Satra turned on his heel and went through the window. Russell looked at his watch, timing it meticulously. When four minutes were up he went to the telephone.

. . . Quite an interesting evening after all.

CHAPTER THREE

Julia Hartley was talking to her editor. Her father was safely in hospital and Charles Russell had asked for time to think. These Tuesday morning conferences were a ritual, partly an assessment of her column on the Sunday before, partly an exchange of ideas for the fresh copy she'd have to deliver on Thursday. It hadn't seemed sensible to cancel the appointment and Julia was a sensible woman.

Her editor was thinking that if Julia Hartley owned a fault it was really that she was too sensible, too civilized. Her marriage had broken down, or had it? Nobody knew, not even Julia. He assumed that they'd given up sleeping together but assumed was the only possible word since their manner in public gave nothing away. The courteous somewhat aloof zoologist, the successful woman journalist. So what do they do when the thing goes wrong? They behave in an elegant adult way : Julia Hartley goes on writing her column and Kendal goes off to the States for a year to some well-paid job which would drive him crazy. And then, after a year, they'd see. The editor suppressed a snort. It was civilized, all right—he gave them that. But he knew that he couldn't have done it himself.

Though he couldn't complain as an editor if Julia seemed a little cool. He paid her to be cool : it sold her column. In the wastes of propaganda, Left and Right, Julia's column in the *Sunday Gong* was an island of simple sanity. She had an unmistakable intelligence but nothing of the bluestocking. A man would not have expected her to be interested in feminism, nor indeed in any other abstraction which plagued the unhappy intellectual. A man would have been right. To Julia Hartley feminism was an ailment of women who had failed in their trade, anything else with an 'ism' on it almost as destructive as a taste for theology. What she wrote had a very personal flavour, not offensively cynical but undeniably realistic. It was her editor's private guess, though never expressed, that more men read her column than women. It made them nod and smile appreciatively. This was a sensible woman, they'd like to meet her.

Many had tried. The editor looked at two trays of unopened letters. 'It seems to have gone down well last Sunday judging from the fan mail.'

'Mary will answer them?'

'Yes, of course.'

Mary was a secretary and she answered Julia's letters politely. She never read them herself and never had, and the editor respected her for it.

'What are you cooking up for next Sunday?'

'Lord Lissdale's been sounding off again.'

'Not a paragraph in my paper—much too dangerous. What Lissdale says in the Lords is right-wing rubbish, but if you printed what he really does we'd have a writ round our ears next morning.'

'I could do it pretty delicately.'

'Not delicately enough for Lissdale's lawyers.'

She struck a line out from her scratch-pad and the editor watched her do it. . . . Fine full figure but not yet stout. Statuesque was the word which came to him. Stately mover but graceful. (Damn it, he was the editor now.) Face surprisingly small, inquiring, decided. And splendid eyes. Long hair still, beautifully kept, for business calls bundled up in a casual pile.

It was the editor's impression that there were possibilities in Julia Hartley. Had Kendal Hartley been very clever? In his job, no doubt, he was quite first class, but there were other things in life than a man's job.

She was asking him now as a casual suggestion: 'A piece about central Europe?'

'But play it cool. We don't blow the outraged liberal trumpet and I doubt if we've yet had the facts which matter.'

'You've heard things, though?'

'I could ask who hasn't.' He looked at her regretfully. 'If there's a story there your father may have it but I know I can't ask you to sniff it out.'

'No, you certainly can't.' Julia said it with conviction. She hadn't even told him what had happened the previous

27

evening. First Charles Russell had asked her not to, and it was a very poor journalist who fouled her own nest.

'But I can't wait to read that book of his.'

She laughed. 'You're a liar but rather a nice one.'

'Well. . . . And the Maidenhair Press—you know what that means. If there'd been anything worth going for somebody like Mackellars they would have snapped it up in an instant.'

'They didn't have a chance, you know. Father didn't use an agent.'

'You mean he went straight to Peregrine Vane?'

'Why not?'

'You know Vane.'

'I only know how keen father is. I don't want him disappointed.'

'Quite. And it's none of my business—the paper is. What were we discussing, please?'

'Not writing a piece about Viscount Lissdale.'

'And possibly writing another on middle Europe.' He reflected, then decided. 'All right then, but down the middle. Moral disapproval is something which ill becomes us here and anyway people are stuffed with it. Moreover, as I said before, I'm sure there's a lot we don't know and never shall.'

She made a brief note. 'And that Bench of hardnosed magistrates down in Sussex?'

'Admirable. The heavies have been giving them stick, calling them reactionaries, brutal barbarians, sadists, the lot. I think myself they acted sensibly. Give us the middle way again, you know how to do it perfectly.'

'I thank you for the compliment. That's all?'

'Two paras is enough?'

'Three's one too many.'

'I must say, you're a pro,' he said.

'I try to give satisfaction.'

'Jesus.'

He watched her sail out, a splendid ship, then went back to his desk and looked at his clock. She'd been businesslike as usual and she'd left him five minutes to kill in thought.

. . . So her husband was in America and when he came back they'd see how it looked. With his mind he approved but his instincts revolted. He'd once been in Kendal Hartley's shoes and he hadn't enjoyed the experience; he'd been bitter and once had beaten her drunkenly, but in its backhanded way the beating had borne at least one fruit : he hadn't won her affection back, on the contrary had increased her indifference, but when she'd finally departed she had left him with a real respect. Of course he'd behaved disgracefully, but then he wasn't a zoologist. Well, somebody had to run newspapers.

He lit up a cigarette, unthinking; he smoked sixty a day and had given up counting. . . . And now Julia had an admirer, he'd heard, a diplomat from behind the Curtain. The poor bastard was buying trouble all right. If he was looking for a casual affair he might not, with Julia Hartley, make it, and if he was serious he was going to burn his fingers badly. A man from another world, another ethos. The editor was sorry for this unfortunate foreign diplomatist.

Not that she'd treat him badly, lead him on. She seemed cool as the Middle West beer he detested, but look how she cared for her father. Outrageous, impossible, pompous man, and Julia gently shielded him, delicately, with a woman's tact. He was her father and that was enough.

Or was he? The editor would have betted against it for he knew all about Agnes Omerod. She'd made a quite disastrous mistake and was entitled to a private life, but the point about private lives was simply privacy. Agnes Omerod, as the habit grew, had been as shameless as an Egyptian queen, her affairs had been long past comment in the society where she'd chosen to live. Which hadn't been diplomatic circles, indeed she'd despised them heartily. She'd seldom gone abroad with Fenton and the editor wasn't surprised at it. Fenton had foreign allowances, Agnes money. Fine. But she needn't have been promiscuous, she needn't have horned him quite so mercilessly. So who was Julia's father, who indeed? The field was a large one, the runners mixed. The editor's private fancy was a Press Baron now in his dotage. He'd been more than a proprietor too; the wretched man could write and well. So could Julia Hartley and Omerod couldn't. This book of his would flop like a stone. There was something called heredity and the editor believed in it.

Did Julia know? It hardly mattered. She was an intelligent woman, perhaps she suspected, and not only from unfriendly gossip. At twenty-eight she must know herself and she hadn't a trait in common with Fenton Omerod. Except the name which he'd given her, and a very cheap price it was for her fierce allegiance. Privately she might laugh at him but nobody else might publicly smile. No man or woman—not in her presence.

The editor blew out smoke and watched it. It struck him as terrible waste but he wasn't offended. And nor was he shy of old-fashioned words. This was loyalty, simple loyalty, and an editor didn't see much of that.

Charles Russell had asked for time to think but he'd been doing much more than just sit and reflect. He'd been busy on the telephone, using a network which still served him gratefully, ringing to men with famous names and to other men with no names at all or if they had them used more than one. Nobody had been definite and nobody could offer proof, but a common thread ran in all the stories. There was more to recent events than the world yet knew.

Charles Russell had been shaken for he had thirty years' experience; he knew how these matters could grow as you slept, a seed in the night, a menacing dark tree next day. Armed men had been moving in middle Europe, tanks across formally friendly frontiers. He'd told Julia Hartley that men of real power seldom acted for ideological motives, but the tanks had rolled and the armed men marched, and in a world of ruthless realists that didn't make sense in isolation. But now there were stories that something had happened, something which hadn't yet been used, and Her Majesty's Ambassador, who'd been there when these secrets were brewing, comes home to a dull retirement and writes a book. He seems extremely cocky about it and he's sold it to the Maidenhair Press. Rightly or wrongly, he still has his diaries and someone has tried a snatch at them.

Charles Russell sighed. There was nothing to go on or nothing concrete, only a situation, but he'd seen far too many in thirty years not to recognize a dangerous one. He'd explained to Julia Hartley that you couldn't act on a single guess but now he had more than a single guess, he had reports from a dozen experienced men. He pulled his still handsome grey moustache, remembering he was now retired. The essence of being an *éminence grise* was to sit back and let them come to you, and Charles Russell wasn't envious of a reputation as a busybody.

So that disposed of formal duty or rather of the lack of it, but Charles Russell, not for the first time, was on the horns. For there was a personal angle he couldn't escape : Julia Hartley who'd served him loyally. And her father's safe held something another man wanted.

Those diaries—he'd seen them. And what had he said to Julia Hartley? 'If there *is* a story it won't be a pretty one. There'll be people who'll want to see it suppressed.' It had been perfectly true as far as it went but he himself had suppressed the corollary. If there were people who wanted this story dead there'd be others who equally wanted it published. It would be justification for what had seemed madness, and from a neutral and therefore convincing source. And these were much more powerful people than were those who wanted the story killed.

Russell looked at the clock : it was half past four. He knew Fenton Omerod was safely in hospital and that Julia Hartley had come up to London. She'd given him a friend's address where she'd said he could catch her at tea time. He dialled the number thoughtfully.

'I've done my thinking for what it's worth. Can you come round for a drink and a chat?'

'I'd like to but I can't this evening. May I come tomorrow morning, early?'

'So you're dining out. He's a lucky man.'

'I don't think myself that he's lucky at all.'

He said softly : 'A foreign diplomat?' Like her editor he had heard of him.

'Charles, you have ass's ears, you really have.' She spoke without rancour, not interested in taking offence. It was something Charles Russell had always admired.

'Not so long as all that. You haven't been furtive.'

'Why the hell should we be furtive?'

'Well, an eminent journalist, one of those embassies—'

A word came down the telephone which the *Sunday Gong* would not have printed.

'Julia, will you answer a question?'

'I worked for you once and I'm coming tomorrow.'

He said on a sudden prick of the thumbs : 'Does anyone else know you're dining with Satra?'

'No. . . . Yes, I mentioned it at the office, I think.'

'To whom?'

'To Mary, she's a secretary. Answers my letters and all that drag. And I have to leave a contact in case anything blows up suddenly. Editor's orders, the price of working for a newspaper.'

'Is she a nice girl—sane politically?'

'I should say she was almost painfully sane.'

She was at this moment ringing her contact. 'Seven-thirty,' she was telling him. 'With Josef Satra as you thought it was. At Prunier's.'

'We'll take care of it.'

CHAPTER FOUR

The Ambassador hadn't much liked it that Satra had failed. He was a fair-minded man where the tenets of his faith were not in question, and Satra's failure had been explicable, even a little unlucky. But it was the absence of luck which worried him, for like many men who thought as he did he was both a rigid determinist and also superstitious in the extreme. His life, he considereed, had taught him one thing : the man attracted events, the luck or its absence. That this was probably heresy had never even occurred to him : he was a hardline communist but he wasn't a philosopher. So Satra had been in the West too long and the West was the world of failure. Naturally he had attracted it, the logic was ineluctable granted the simple premises.

Satra was saying heavily : 'I'm sorry I didn't bring it off.'

'The failure was unfortunate.' The tone was reasonable but implied no concession. 'Meanwhile I've a normal job for you.' His Excellency indulged a half-smile. 'No, nothing to do with the major matter; I could hardly use you in that again. It's to do with this Week which we're running in Guildford.'

'And which you're opening this afternoon.'

'Which I was going to open this afternoon. Now I find I can't face it.'

'You haven't been looking well of late.'

'That puts it in a most English way.' The Ambassador didn't show his thoughts but again they'd begun to trouble him. The understatement had been quite unconscious but also it was characteristic. This man was becoming extremely English. A trifle? But trifles counted.

'I know you suffer a lot of pain.'

'For a fortnight I haven't been free of it and I'm not as young as I once was. But we've put in a lot of work on this Week, and besides the rubbish we hope to sell it's going to bring us a good deal of sympathy. Brave little Belgium, gutsy our country. Business as usual—I know the English. So we'll have to send someone to show the flag properly.'

'It's opening in a big store, I've heard, at half past four to catch the rush. You want me to go with the Commercial Counsellor?'

'No, I want you to go without him, to read my speech.'

Satra didn't hide astonishment. 'Morava won't like the idea at all.'

'I can deal with Morava.'

'May I ask your reasons?'

'By all means, since you should certainly know them. It's primarily a women's store. Take a look at Morava, then one in the mirror. You might not succeed in Hollywood—no. For one thing you're much too taut and they like them relaxed. You're not even classically handsome but you've got something which Morava hasn't. And plenty of it, believe an old man. I told you it was a woman's shop.'

'You surprise me, sir.'

'I don't see why. Well, here's the speech.' He passed it over but not quite happily. Josef Satra wasn't ideal for the job for the English didn't like taking it straight, they liked the occasional laugh as seasoning. Josef Satra wouldn't give them that, he would no more jest than take wings to the moon. Perhaps it didn't matter, though : he had something the English would also recognize, a total unquestioning dedication.

So the Ambassador passed his speech over quickly. 'Don't try to memorize, that kills it dead. Just memorize what each paragraph says, then use your own words as they come to you. Go carefully with the fiddly bits.'

'What fiddly bits?'

'The sob stuff which I hated writing, the appeals to English sympathy which we both of us despise. But if I say so myself they're beautifully controlled.'

'Then I hope I can control them.'

'So do I.'

Now Satra was driving to Guildford fast. If he hadn't been competent he wouldn't have driven, taking the embassy chauffeur instead. What you did well you did yourself, but if there were any doubt of it you sent for a man with established skills. He'd been taught that all his forty years and by now it was second nature.

For Russell had guessed right about his age. He'd been a boy when Hitler had seized his country and a youth of eighteen when its communists had come to power. He'd always secretly sympathized, less because doctrine had gripped his guts than because he saw no future in the frailties of a democracy. His country was an island in a land mass of other and hostile races, a standing temptation to greater powers. It couldn't survive by playing them off— that had been tried in the past and failed. What it needed was an ally and your major ally exacted his price. The latest one had been far too high.

So he'd been doing his national service when the communists had taken over and at once he'd openly joined the Party. Before it would have been dangerous, a conscript soldier under officers he mistrusted, and Satra had all the dour caution of his race. But now it was safe as well as sensible and soon it had paid him dividends lushly. They'd commissioned him—there were vacancies in hundreds now— and he'd served as a regimental soldier. Then there'd been courses and finally that special one. Two years in the States under final training, then another year in Sweden. He'd

34

hated Sweden and the smug Swedes. Now he was in London as the Military Attaché.

He would have thought you unsophisticated if you'd considered him any sort of agent; he thought of his work as entirely legitimate and when he'd been sent to Omerod's house his instinct had been to protest to the limit. In the end he'd obeyed what had been put as an order but he hadn't been in the least surprised when the mission had gone sour on him. It hadn't been his official trade which was simply to keep his eyes open. And surprisingly easy he'd always found it. Almost everything was in print somewhere if you only found out where to dig it up, and when there was any sort of doubt they invited you to their War Games. At first he'd thought it a clever front, an elaborate English sham to hide what mattered. Incredulously he had learned it wasn't. He watched as he'd been trained to watch and his first-class reports had been welcomed and praised. He realized he was well thought of and had hopes for his next promotion. Even back to the States as Number One. . . .

He grunted in disquiet as he drove. And this was the promising diplomat who had fallen hard for Julia Hartley. He corrected the thought with the discipline they'd taught him. Not 'fallen' since that went much too far. A man who had fallen was besotted beyond hope or pride and he wasn't yet that or anything like it; he was simply a man in a blank dilemma. Julia Hartley wouldn't follow him but nor could he stay in Julia's country. He could defect, no doubt, but even the thought made him sweat in shame. It offended him as a soldier and it outraged him as a patriot. He wouldn't do that for a woman—never. Besides, she wasn't his woman or anywhere near it. She still wore a wedding ring and had been perfectly, even brutally, frank. She and Kendal Hartley had come to a crisis as others had too, so she was keeping her work for a year at least and Kendal had taken a job in the States. When he came back they'd see what happened.

It had struck him as very English indeed but he hadn't quite disapproved of it. It was better than premature divorce : he'd seen dozens in the States and had thought them silly. It was better than throwing the crockery, better than using fists or nails; above all it was better than bitter-

35

ness. Julia Hartley wasn't a bitter woman but it was clear that she wasn't a happy one. She had told him the story as cool as you please but it was certain she wasn't proud of it.

He wondered what she thought of him apart from his masculinity. False modesty was a bourgeois vice and he could see that he attracted her. They'd first met when she'd come to stay with her father, and in the pretentious little embassy, her own aura tainted by Fenton Omerod's, he hadn't paid special attention. Nor had he sought her out in London, but their worlds often crossed and inevitably they had met again. So what did she think of him, *how* did she think? He'd assumed at first that she'd seen him as potential copy, but she'd never asked him about his work or even mentioned it. And she seemed happy in his increasing company, friendly, relaxed, but never more. She'd never refused an invitation.

But she couldn't be that cool, it wouldn't make sense; she had dozens of friends and other admirers. As an escort he was presentable but by no means a trophy to hang on the wall, even if she'd been scalp-hunting which he was perfectly sure she never did. And as anything even faintly serious Josef Satra would be unpromising. A foreigner from behind the Curtain, rather a dim corner at that. What would an upper-crust English girl think of the race from which he sprang? She was educated so she'd know its history. They weren't exactly romantic, hardly dashing. They'd staffed the middle-piece civil service ranks of Maria Theresa's crazy empire but very few had gone to the top. Why should they go to the top indeed when the men in Vienna considered them peasants? No Austrian or Hungarian family would have happily married a daughter to Satra, and why again should they when he had nothing to offer of elegance? Only the simple essential virtues. His people could boast of two well-known composers but neither of unquestioned first rank, no major painter, no writers but the depressingly earnest. They were really the Celts of central Europe, the people you pushed remorselessly westwards, out onto the periphery—Brittany, Cornwall, Ireland, the Isles. Since that hadn't been possible they'd been quietly encircled, sometimes ignored and more often exploited, surrounded by races more

36

gifted and gayer or simply by peoples much better at war. Julia Hartley would know most of this but she'd never refused his invitation. She was dining with him tonight come to that, and it was going to be quite close timing to make it.

He drove into Guildford and found his store, leaving the car in the garage below it. He'd had a pass for that with His Excellency's speech, and the latter he'd studied carefully. He was glad to have done so since it was quite a big function, more formal than he'd been warned or expected and very much better attended. They had cleared a whole department and the local fathers were there in regalia, his national flag behind the dais, perhaps four hundred people on small hard chairs. Morava, the Commercial Counsellor, had put in a lot of work on this Week; he'd been very disappointed that the Ambassador hadn't been able to come and more than a little put out that he wasn't the stand-in. Just the same, Satra thought, His Excellency had been right again. Out of every six present five were women, and Morava, for all his virtues, had let himself go.

He made his speech carefully, following the advice given him, using the Ambassador's points but the words which came most naturally. At first they just listened politely, then he suddenly realized he had them. He had seldom spoken in public before and then only on matters technical, but only a fool could have failed to sense what came up at him out of the audience. It was sympathy for his theme at first but later empathy with the speaker. At the end they clapped and some even cheered. The mayor wrung his hand and led him off.

He was disturbed to find that they'd laid on a party. It was six o'clock, there'd been other speeches. Now there'd be thirty-five minutes at least to be modest and smile socially. His appointment was for half past seven so he was going to have to step on it.

He escaped when he decently could and went down in the lift to the basement garage. His car was almost the last one left since parking had been by ticket only. Such as remained were already moving. Satra climbed in and felt for the starter and a man rapped on the window sharply.

Josef Satra looked up, a little annoyed. He was pressed enough already without the need to explain to a stranger

37

that he didn't much fancy giving lifts. But the man didn't seem to want a lift, he seemed to be some kind of walker, with rucksack and beard and ill-kept boots. He was holding a map and pointing to it, gesticulating.

Satra reluctantly wound down the window. The man held the map out, pointing again.

'I'm lost, can you help me?'

'We're in Guildford, that's all I know. These aren't my parts, I'm not even English.'

'I guessed that from the C.D. plate.'

Satra looked at the man again. He had an excellent ear for the English tongue and this tramper's accent belied his boots. He wore a deplorable hat pulled down low on the forehead and dark glasses which didn't quite hide hard eyes. An instinctive bell of warning rang sharply, but Josef Satra suppressed it crossly. He wasn't some nervous suburban housewife.

'Where do you want to go, then?'

'To Farnham.'

'That's straight across the Hog's Back, I think.'

'But I've broken my glasses. Can't you show me?' He started to spread the map on the bonnet.

Satra cursed but got out. He leant down across the bonnet too and the stranger straightened suddenly. Satra never even saw it coming.

The tramper looked round the garage carefully. It was empty now and he picked up Satra. He'd slipped down from the bonnet without a sound but the tramper handled him easily. He dumped him in the back of the car and stood checking it over methodically. . . . Put him out for an hour, they'd told him—nothing worse. Well, he'd taken a packet; he'd last for rather longer than that. And they'd told him something else so he did it. He took Satra's wallet, his cigarette case, his watch.

He stepped back and gave a final look. Major Josef Satra was going to be late.

CHAPTER FIVE

His Excellency the Ambassador had been reading his latest instructions from home, his fine old face rigid and grey with worry. To begin with they were a reprimand, and that was something he'd never expected. Not because he was an Excellency, since he was far too steeped in his Party's ways to suppose that a mere Ambassador made real policy, but because he'd served his Party well, never quite at the top but always trusted. And here were men who might well be his sons berating him like a novice member. . . . He'd reported some disquiet about his Military Attaché, whom he hinted had been too long in the West. Very right, very proper as far as it went. But what does he do with this Josef Satra—have him watched as he had the means to do? Not at all. He sends him on a most delicate mission, one in any case for professionals. The wording didn't put it so bluntly but that had been really outrageous bad judgment. There was even a hint he'd gone soft himself, that he'd been hoping for a cheap success, something he could report in Satra's favour. This was the deadliest flick of all for he couldn't entirely deny it. He liked Josef Satra, or more accurately he valued his virtues; he'd be very distressed indeed if the West unmanned him. So he'd sent him on a mission when by all the books he shouldn't, and the mission had failed as such missions did. His Excellency, as the simple result, was now looking at a reprimand. It didn't too much impress him for he wasn't an ambitious man, and he suspected he hadn't much longer to live. They could recall him and he'd accept at once, he'd even be pleased to die at home. But not in disgrace after all these years, not mistrusted, an ageing failure.

He turned to the rest of the long dispatch, reading with mounting anxiety. It had been delivered by the weekly courier. He'd guessed that Fenton Omerod had somehow stumbled on something discreditable, and good patriot that he was he'd wished to kill it. But it was very much more serious than anything simply discreditable; it was something to blow his country apart, to end what was left of its independence. He'd been thinking in terms of foolish men, a generation gone soft through lack of struggle, young people bemused with weak Western ideas—a free Press, opposition, the secret ballot. Ach! These were decadent toys for decadent children and he hadn't wished fresh publicity in an English book. That period was finished now, the children had paid, they'd all of them paid. Foreign tanks sat in their laagers outside the cities.

They wouldn't sit passive for long if this news were true.

He re-read the paragraph for at first he hadn't believed it. There'd been much more than Westward leanings and false ideas: there'd been talk of a loan and more than talk, there'd been the first and most delicate soundings. Fenton Omerod had been the go-between—they didn't yet know whether authorized or privately. A huge loan from a Western consortium, a new industrial complex in a province still German at heart though it didn't now speak it. Oh God, if you live still, spare us that. For they wouldn't remain in discreet cantonments if they knew what this dreadful dispatch was telling him. They'd have been justified and they'd bawl it triumphantly; they'd have proof of the worst from a neutral source, something they'd probably scented before but hadn't been able to raise as a banner. So an end to the rags of independence—military occupation, blood in the streets. A secret police which could now work openly, beatings and deaths which were never reported. And mass deportations—he feared those most. The old man snarled. Fenton Omerod held the fuse to the powder and he proposed to light it cold-bloodedly. Not a thought for the people he knew must suffer but a best-selling book and a quick notoriety.

Sir Fenton would do this over his body and body was a serious thought. He could walk into Omerod's hospital and put a bullet in his repellent head. He hadn't a great deal of life before him, and only a bourgeois moralist would think of the act as vulgar murder. It would be justice, natural justice, and a fine way to go out at that. For naturally there'd be more than one shot, no stupid trial of a mad Ambassador.

But as his anger cooled his brain took over. There'd be a sensation too which he'd learned to loathe, and every sort of probe and inquiry. He wouldn't be there as the principal actor and the Foreign Office would reach for the white-wash, but the British Press would smell a story and he'd a solid respect for the British Press. Moreover, killing an author wouldn't be final. The book would remain and the diaries behind it. The Maidenhair Press was intending to publish and Omerod's diaries were still the backing. An attempt had been made to steal them and failed.

. . . Publish—what did that mean? A man wrote a book and he offered it to a publisher, then they entered into a contract which it was better not to think about. The author, if he was a new one, would be unreasonably excited, and the publisher, if experienced, would be quietly keeping his fingers crossed. He'd accepted a risk, he'd been offered one. But if the offer were withdrawn, what then? There'd be a contract, legally binding no doubt, but would a reputable firm impose its rights if its author were on written record that he didn't wish publication after all? Then there'd be letters to major newspapers on the writing paper of Pall Mall clubs, even a spot on telly if the outraged author was well enough known. Omerod wasn't a well-known author but he was an ex-Ambassador. Would a publisher think the fuss worth while? His Excellency couldn't be sure but he doubted that Vane would risk it. The conclusion was there-fore evident: Omerod was the key, not Vane. If Omerod withdrew this appalling book. . . .

If Omerod could be forced to, frightened. . . .

The lined face relaxed as the brain worked smoothly. It was a matter he'd sometimes handled before, simply forcing a man to do something he otherwise wouldn't. For a hard-liner that was orthodox, even classical, thinking. The Am-bassador had been other things before they'd turned him into an errand boy and now he was on familiar ground, his thinking logical, the conclusion in his Party's mainstream. Pressure first, but what pressure? Blackmail? He hadn't a lever. So much the better, that made it simpler. Even black-mail had been known to fail, but one thing had never failed and it never would. You put the fear of God in a man, you put the fear of death into Fenton Omerod. Don't publish that book because if you do. . . . And not just threats since he might not believe them. The medicine must be produced and tasted. His Excellency had met Sir Fenton and he didn't think courage was one of his virtues. The courier had gone home by air but the Ambassador wrote a message in highest cipher.

The answer came back with a comforting promptitude and the Ambassador, comforted, nodded approvingly. They'd think that he'd taken a grip of himself with this plan which came straight from a well-thumbed book. They wouldn't have had to think or weigh it, only to look for the precedents. God knew there were plenty of them to find.

He read the last line of the answer again. The man he had asked for was already on an aircraft. Passport in order, spoke English, not known.

He smiled again—they were still efficient. Whether their actions were still secure, as secret as once they had been, he doubted.

His doubts were in fact entirely justified. His codes had been broken for several weeks, his messages copied and quietly passed on. They were copied to where he would least have wished.

Julia Hartley was sitting in Prunier's waiting, drinking Campari since she didn't like gin. It was five to eight and she was becoming a little anxious. She wasn't a woman to feel diminished because an escort was half an hour late to meet her and she knew he worked hard and irregular hours, which, she suspected, most Attachés did not. But she couldn't sit drinking Campari for ever, blocking a table which the restaurant could fill easily. The head waiter had started to hover uncomfortably.

She was conscious of a tall man with the easy assurance of certain status. 'Good evening,' he said, 'you seem to have been kept waiting. May I sit down and fill in for a moment?'

'Please do.' She didn't much care for Lissdale but at least he was male, he would regularize that empty chair till Josef Satra arrived to claim it. She watched him order a pink gin gracefully, thinking that in his way he was quite a man. Her editor had just turned him down as a subject for comment in Sunday papers, and as a journalist she wasn't surprised. He had first-class lawyers and marvellous cover. The two went hand in hand together, for the former protected the latter dourly.

He was a Tory peer, the ninth in line, and he talked rubbish in the House of Lords. Quite a few of his nominal party agreed but none of them thought it discreet to say so. Lord Lissdale had read the Marxist canon, and he didn't dissent from the premises, not at all. There *was* a class war, you could see it everywhere, but the logic from that point was far from conclusive. Why should the proletariat come out top? The intellectuals seemed to think it would and were scurrying in to make their peace, but that, to Lord Lissdale, seemed premature. So there was a war but far from a lost one, and the enemy was the working class. Then why not accept it and act accordingly? He did himself. One of the companies whose board he was on for his ancient name had been considering a new factory. It had been viable too and might well make them money, but it would also create five thousand jobs in an area where unemployment was high. So he'd persuaded his board not to build the factory. Of course not—there was a war on, class war.

He'd been frothing on this in the House of Lords, a possible subject for Julia's column till her editor had sat on it. Wisely, she'd admitted, since it wasn't what was interesting. What Lissdale said in the Other Place was a blackish joke and extreme old hat : the real news was what His Lordship did, and they couldn't print that. They didn't dare.

For Lord Lissdale's outrageous politics were a smoke-screen and an effective cloak. He was a clever man in his tangled way, not intellectual-clever but just plain smart; he'd written a good biography and been a history don before he'd been Lissdale, and he'd learnt one of history's lessons quickly. This was that when The Day arrived—something which as a committed communist he couldn't and didn't doubt for a moment—the ragbag which thought itself heirs apparent would certainly be no such thing. Not the fellow-travellers, the progressives and permissives, the professors of literature who wrote so unsyntactically, the tedious female

43

broadcasters with voices which set your teeth on edge. All these would go to the labour camps first and Lord Lissdale wouldn't regret them. For really they were extremely stupid. Nothing taught them the obvious lesson—nothing. Not even Czechoslovakia.

Lord Lissdale carried no party card since members of consequence seldom did; Lord Lissdale was used when they needed a smoothie. All Fleet Street knew this and most politicians. The one couldn't print it, the other say so. Lissdale had very good lawyers indeed, but one day he wouldn't need lawyers at all for he'd be very much more than a simple agent. Or so Lord Lissdale sincerely believed. Meanwhile he served on contentedly, as secure in the knowledge of final reward as any Christian in his ultimate heaven. He was a happy man but very dangerous.

'Your host is late,' he told Julia coolly.

'Yes, I've a date, or I thought I had.'

'Then I'm the fortunate man, it seems.'

In fact there had been no fortune at all. Lord Lissdale had acted urgently for his orders had been extremely urgent. There was mischief planned against Fenton Omerod and that mischief would come in the small hours if not prevented. Prevented it would certainly be, but the danger thereafter was misunderstanding, that Security would misread events and call down its still quite powerful fire on what would be a mistaken target. On the precedents and on all past form that target would be Lord Lissdale's masters, who till Charles Russell retired could have reached him directly. The new man was not in that league just yet so Russell must hear from a source he'd credit, when he'd contact the Executive with all the great weight of his private prestige, avoiding thereby what was always disastrous, a confusion or false assessment of interests. Julia Hartley would be an excellent channel : she was Omerod's daughter and had once worked for Russell, and she was dining with Josef Satrà that evening, or rather she had been but now she wouldn't. That had all been arranged and perfectly simply. It would be made to look like a coshing and robbery and Lord Lissdale would seize the moment offered.

... Tonight? Yes, tonight. Lord Lissdale must realize that

time was essential. If you wanted a message to stick and be acted on, you gave it before events, not after. There was a difference and a vital one between a warning and an explanation.

Lissdale looked at his watch. 'It's getting late.'

'And the waiter is getting restive.'

'So I can see.' He smiled at her, showing excellent teeth. 'I suppose you wouldn't let me order?'

'I don't see why not since you're sitting there, but I warn you I'm pretty hungry.'

'I think I can just afford it. You know where most of the money comes from.' This time he laughed and called the waiter. The waiter came up immediately, beaming and barely hiding relief. Like all good waiters he hated irregularity and a woman sitting alone too long was irregular and maybe worse.

Lissdale didn't look at him. 'Sole,' he said, 'to start with, of course, and please forget the more tiresome trimmings. Then saddle of lamb with peas and no potatoes. After that we can think again.' He looked at Julia. 'I hope that suits you?'

'Perfectly, thank you.'

'A Vouvray with the sole, I suggest.' He was talking to the *sommelier* now. 'And after that the claret you gave me last week. It was very expensive for what it was but it wasn't a bad drink at all.'

'With pleasure, my lord.'

'I'm not a life peer so you don't have to use it.'

Julia laughed but checked it. 'You're rather a complex character.'

'Not at all. I'm really extremely simple at heart. I have to be.'

'I realize that.'

'But I do have certain humble uses, such as picking up charming women and giving them warnings.'

'Warnings?'

'It's the simplest word and therefore the best.'

'But a warning about what?' she asked.

'A warning about your father's book.'

She was puzzled and said so.

45

'It fits together perfectly simply if you care to put your mind to it. Your father is writing a book?'

'You know it.'

'And he's just come out of a country which I don't think I want to mention?'

She nodded.

'He's very confident the book will succeed?' He didn't wait for an answer. 'Well, there you are.'

'I'm not there at all, you're telling me nothing.'

He looked at her, his face a sudden mask of contempt; he had pale blue eyes under hooded lids. 'Please don't fool with me.'

'Very well then, I'll concede you this. If that book does have something it's something hot.'

'It's very hot indeed,' he said.

'And you're telling me you want it suppressed?'

'On the contrary we want it published. *We want it published at any price.*'

She thought it over quickly, eating the sole. 'Do you want to know how it strikes me?'

'That's the idea.'

'Then if the people you work for want it published there'll be a country which most certainly doesn't.'

'Quite. So the hypothesis we're now agreed on is that one country would like the book suppressed. *Ergo* they'll try to suppress it.'

'How?'

He poured her more wine though he could see that the wine waiter disapproved. Lord Lissdale was unimpressed by wine waiters. 'Your father . . .' he said softly.

She tautened at once. Up to now they'd been playing a sort of game and Julia had been enjoying it. Now it was suddenly serious—Lissdale was serious.

'I can see that you're not really believing me, but you don't know my world as I do. Journalists often think they do and they certainly know it better than most, but when it comes down to the cold reality—'

'What are you trying to tell me?'

'That the book is your father's, that your father owns the copyright.'

'And somebody wants him to call it back. Is that the warning?'

'It is indeed. But I can offer you rather more than a warning, you and your useful friend Charles Russell. I can offer some reassurance too.' He drank some claret. 'It's still a matter of logic, you see. There are people who want to *protect* that book and they're very powerful people indeed. I should know that.'

'What are you trying to tell me this time?'

'The truth. Any pressure against your father would most certainly be resisted.'

'How could it be resisted?'

'By the exercise of a little foresight. Specifically, by breaking ciphers.'

'But my father's still in hospital.'

'Rest assured that we're aware of it.'

'I don't know what to make of all this.' She was puzzled again and sounded it.

'You don't have to make, you just listen and remember. If you also pass on to Russell we'd be obliged. I was told to give you a message and I have. A glass of brandy?'

'I need it.'

They drank their brandy and he signalled to the waiter again, initialling the bill boldly with a single capital L. He saw her into a cab politely and she watched him walk up St James's and into Boodle's.

Back in the flat her friend was asleep and she began to get ready for bed herself, glancing idly at forwarded letters. Then she pulled out an envelope quickly, the writing known. It was a letter from Kendal Hartley, her husband.

She stood holding it uncertainly. There'd been no firm arrangement for writing letters—perhaps they'd write and perhaps they wouldn't—and now that she came to think of it there'd been no firm arrangement for anything. The agreement they'd reached had been almost unspoken, a treaty by default or perhaps just an armistice. He'd go abroad for a year and then they'd see.

She opened the letter with a sudden quick tear and began to read it avidly. He wrote extremely well, she knew, for he wasn't the sort of scientist who preferred to think in

47

symbols. He used language very expertly, an elegant patina on disciplined thought. It was an admirable letter but it told her almost nothing of what a woman would wish to know. . . . He was well and getting used to the food, though at first there'd been too much starch, too many of everything. The Americans ate enormously, and what a city threw away would feed a country. He had very pleasant lodgings but not quite the work he'd been led to expect. His university was researching on some project for the military, and though it seemed harmless he wasn't sure. There was a faint but quite definite smell and he didn't like it. He hoped she was well and her column flourishing. But of course it was. He really didn't need to ask it.

It was a friendly little letter but in its way it was infuriating. She saw there was a postscript which wasn't typical. The wording, though, was.

I hope you won't think it brash of me but I've sent on a little parcel. The posts are quite unpredictable, so it may not arrive with this letter which covers it.

She saw that it had and opened it. It was a bottle of very expensive scent and it happened to be her favourite.

She got into bed but not using the scent. After all, she thought sourly, why should she alone? But she was glad that he had thought of her, gladder still he'd remembered her preference.

Kendal Hartley could make you very cross but whatever his failings he wasn't stupid.

Russell listened next morning in total silence, then gave her a second cup of coffee. She watched him as she drank it slowly. She knew he was sixty, he didn't show it. His lean jaw had been carefully shaven, the long grey head was as carefully brushed; he'd been eating an English breakfast but his waist was still as trim as a boy's. He said at last:

'Do you mind if we recap a bit?'

'Please do.'

'Then the first stage as I see it is that somebody tries for your father's diaries. We don't know who it was and we

48

shan't find out. The police haven't a hope in a case like that.'
He cocked an inquiring eyebrow. 'Agreed?'

'That's perfectly right as far as it goes.'

'Then the second stage, though not chronologically, is
when Satra rang you early this morning. You were dining
with him last night but he didn't turn up. I'd like to hear
what he said again.'

'He told me he'd been coshed and robbed. At Guildford
where he'd gone down for their Week. He sounded very
ashamed of himself.'

'You believed him?'

'Why not? And he did sound upset, and shaken too.'

'Yes. . . . Be that as it may he didn't turn up. Lord Lissdale did, though, and Lissdale talked. We'll call that the
third stage. We both of us know about Lissdale and Lissdale
talked.'

'He talked in elliptic parables but I think I got the message.'

'So have I but rather a different one. It's one I've had
several times before when I was sitting at a certain desk and
two very big boys were fighting a private battle on what
happened to be my territory.' He lit a cigar and smiled at
her. 'KEEP OUT', he said in capitals, 'that was the message
through you to me. Your country may have an interest here
but it's indirect and much less than ours.'

She said a little tentatively since he knew these difficult
waters and she did not : 'But surely the Executive—'

'No, it isn't yet ripe for the Security Executive. The
Executive are counter-punchers and there's nothing concrete
for them to counter-punch. Whatever may lie behind Lissdale's talk it's something extremely political, and I haven't
yet got the feel of it, not the real smell. But I'll talk to Harry
Tuke, I think. He's got an excellent head and we're still good
friends.'

'You think Lissdale was serious?'

'Yes, I do.'

'He rather more than hinted that his friends might be taking a hand in this. You think they would?'

'I know they *could*.'

The telephone rang and Russell answered. 'Yes,' he said,

'I'll tell her,' and put it down. 'They rang your house early this morning but the servants hadn't arrived when they called. When they rang again a few minutes ago they were given your London number. It was lucky you told your friend you were here.'

'And who's the mysterious "they", please?' She was interested but not excited. It was probably only her newspaper.

'They were your father's hospital. There's been, well, an incident.'

She asked on a gasp: 'It's serious?'

'They asked you to go there urgently. I'll drive you down at once if you're ready.'

'He's alive?'

'I don't know.'

CHAPTER SIX

Sir Fenton in his hospital had been visited by another knight, but this time one who had earned his honour. Sir Albert Bull, whom Omerod hated, was Permanent Under-Secretary, head of the Foreign Service. He was a remarkable man in a remarkable appointment. Only a few years ago and an Albert Bull in this powerful seat would have been totally unimaginable, since he had neither the aura and far less the background for what up to then had been thought of as diplomacy. That was the reason a shrewd Prime Minister had picked him over the heads of others. There'd been several resignations which had been happily accepted. The Prime Minister had mistrusted these men and Bull had been content enough that he wouldn't be embarrassed by their presence as his subordinates.

He was the son of a country solicitor who had fought his way up the ladder by brains and guts, first a scholarship to a scholars' school, then to Oxford and the Indian Civil. He'd transferred to the Political, then, when India had folded up on him, been recruited into the Foreign Service. He'd always been efficient, confident he'd rise reasonably high, but he'd never expected the desk he now filled. It had taken him just a fortnight to discover why he'd been put in it.

What a mess, what a stinking stable! It wasn't important nowadays that Her Majesty's representatives were second-rate men : an Ambassador was an errand boy, liable at the first hint of troube to find a Minister on his extravagant doorstep or at least a coded telegram which left him with no discretion whatever. Albert Bull thought this unimportant and indeed he rather welcomed it, but the Foreign Office was more than ambassadors; it was a great Department of State in Whitehall.

Great it might have once been but it wasn't now. To the Press it was a boring joke, a place where one went for the standard hand-outs. If men wanted to know about Czechoslovakia they went to the Board of Trade or the Treasury, to the Ministry of Midwives, anywhere. Anywhere but to the Foreign Office. It was bad when the public image was wet, even worse when the private image was wetter. For the other Departments despised you and barely hid it. The airs and graces were resented, and there wasn't the cool efficiency which made airs and graces acceptable. Those terrible briefs for Ministers. You put them up to stonewall dourly, then threw away their wickets when the barracking became too noisy. It had happened too often and then again, and the other Departments had laughed their heads off. Being a Foreign Office Junior Minister was a form of political suicide.

Albert Bull, in six months, had done a good deal, wielding the axe with skill and ruthlessly. He'd had regulations which let him do so, for unlike the civil service proper a Foreign Servant could be put out to grass and he couldn't claim another post. The paddocks of upper suburbia were full of these ageing resentful nags, the well-connected nonentities, the clubmen, the Fenton Omerods.

Fenton Omerod—now there was a right bastard. You'd have thought he'd go quieter than most since he didn't need money. His wife had left him that if nothing else. Perhaps it made up and perhaps it didn't—everyone knew about Agnes Omerod. So there he was in his splendid villa, nursing resentment, brewing up bitterness. And he was writing another silly book.

But though Omerod might be writing rubbish it simply hadn't occurred to Bull that he could also act improperly. A strict man himself, he gave even the stupidest credit for knowing the rules which bound them. Bull hadn't even thought of a scandal since he didn't consider Omerod scandalous : what he feared was further embarrassment, the echo of mocking laughter again. There'd been a recent spate of diplomats' memoirs and the Office wasn't yet in shape for another dose of ridicule. What terrible tripe the books had been, how appallingly illuminating in exactly the way Albert Bull didn't want. There were good men still in the mannered rabble and some young ones who were promising, but these memoirs had been very old hat, the books of the last of the cocktail diplomatists. The Office couldn't stand for another with its image what it already was.

Albert Bull had considered the problem carefully, then had put on his hat and gone down to Omerod's hospital. He knew he'd been mugged by a burglar and he thought it a pity he hadn't hit harder. Bull was a forthright man and he never pretended; he didn't like Fenton Omerod so he wouldn't affect a sympathy which he didn't feel.

And the interview hadn't gone well at all. Albert Bull resented patronage and he resented it especially when it was totally unjustified. He knew all about Fenton Omerod : both men were from sound if modest backgrounds, but Fenton had spent a lifetime learning a part and Albert hadn't. Sir Fenton indeed! His name had been William. So now he came upper crust at you and Albert Bull, a fair-minded man, would have admitted he did it beautifully. This he rightly resented but it also wrong-footed him. For the only appeal he could make to Omerod was the classic one, how-ever corny—the Service and its traditions, the public good, what was and was not done amongst an *élite*. Fine—but not coming from Albert Bull. Who knew what Omerod thought of him perfectly; he thought of him as an upstart, perhaps even as a usurper. It wasn't quite incredible that Omerod had secretly hoped for Sir Albert's job. It was incredible that he'd ever have got it, even under a dispensation dead and buried, but it wasn't at all incredible that Omerod should have harboured the thought. He was a very ambitious man indeed and he'd spent a whole lifetime nursing ambition.

Bull hung his hat up and played out his hand. He knew it wasn't impressive so he played it out for what it was worth. He was an excellent negotiator so he didn't attempt finesses against the odds.

'I've come about this book of yours.'

Omerod ignored it. 'How pleasant it is to see you again.' Timing it like a professional actor he slid a glance at the table beside his bed. It was piled with books and flowers and fruit.

. . . Rather well done. He's conveying I should have brought him something. One up to Fenton Omerod.

'We've had three or four books of memoirs and all of them were quite disastrous. All of them painted pictures of a world which is long since dead and gone. I wouldn't object to that in the least if they'd also troubled to make it clear that that world *is* dead and gone for ever. What I don't like the public thinking is that foreign affairs are still run that way.'

'I take your point, it's perfectly clear.'

. . . If I were a duke's grandson he'd be agreeing at once, all over me.

'So putting it in the newest manner, I'd be glad if your book didn't add to the list.'

'I understood that several minutes ago.'

Sir Albert Bull sighed. He still had a card though it wasn't a good one. 'I gather the Maidenhair Press is doing it?'

'Yes, I was fortunate.'

'But they're not exactly a leading firm.'

'If you mean they're not the biggest or richest—yes. But they have something uncommercial and to me that's rather important.'

'I see. . . . Will they sell your book?'

'Oh yes, I think so.'

'None of those others sold well at all.'

Fenton Omerod said with an utter certainty: 'But this one will.'

The man with the passport in order and excellent English, not known to the English police nor Security, climbed out of his aircraft and went through Customs. He met with no hitch of any kind except one which he wasn't aware of. An inconspicuous man had been warned to expect him and he followed him to his waiting car. It was a hire service car but that was natural. Anything else would simply have been careless. The inconspicuous man watched it drive away, then went into a phone box quickly. The line was a public one and he treated it accordingly.

'Our friend has arrived,' he said, 'alone.'

'No trouble with Customs or Passports?'

'No.'

'You're sure it was he?'

'He tallied with the photograph. Clever of you to get it in time.'

'Once we know of an interesting visitor coming his reception is mere routine, my friend. You heard where he told his driver to go?'

'Only the name of the town. In Surrey.'

'That's good enough to alert Delivery.'

'For the package of goods we suppose he's collecting?'

'Yes. Just so.'

'You're not expecting difficulty?'

'None. Nor will our friend be. That's the point.'

'The deliverer knows what to do?'

'Indeed.'

The man said unexpectedly : 'For Chrissake don't let her kill him.'

'Be more careful.'

The voice rang off.

Albert Bull hadn't reached his present rank without a first class flair for reading men and much experience of mankind to whet the gift. But he wasn't quite infallible and knew more than enough of the hairless ape to know that you couldn't be sure of the beast. His assessment of Fenton Omerod had been accurate as far as it went but it hadn't been quite inclusive. The man was a sort of dinosaur, a survival from another age, magnificent in its reptilian way but distressingly out of date in the modern world. He hadn't been born a dinosaur either, but had made himself into the perfect replica. That had lacked foresight and common judgment, and naturally Omerod had paid the price; he'd been Ambassador in a second-class State and that had been the end of him. Of course he was disappointed and bitter : Bull would have been astonished if he were not. All this he saw instinctively, but his instincts weren't quite acute enough to sense what was driving Fenton Omerod. The word for it by now was malice.

Omerod had watched him leave the hospital, wiping him from his mind without effort. He was good at wiping people out—any diplomat had to be good at that if he were going to survive in sanity. Besides, Bull was irrelevant. Fenton Omerod saw it perfectly clearly. He detested Albert Bull as a man but if it hadn't been Bull they'd have found another. It wasn't that common Bull who'd betrayed him. It was the system.

He moved uneasily in his hospital bed. It was a private room but the bed was dubious. . . . Betrayed—it was the only word. You sqaundered your manhood in unquestioning service, in blind worship of the god you'd chosen, and when you came near to the top of the queue he laughed in your adoring face. The god had changed and you'd wasted your life. Albert Bull had been right in one thing, though. Fenton Omerod was a disciplined man, but his loyalty went to a system not to men. When that had crashed he was quite without scruple.

He lit a cigar and watched the smoke. . . Albert Bull was Grade 1 and he'd never made that. He mightn't have got Bull's desk perhaps, but he ought to have gone very near to it. After that spell in middle Europe he'd hoped to be a Deputy, Deputy Under-Secretary of State. There were six of those, though God knew why, and from that springboard one might go anywhere, to one of the really important posts if some wretched politician didn't scandalously usurp it. The ambition had been high but not unreasonable, even a few years ago its fulfilment a very fair bet indeed. And then Helbert and Willis-Price had gone over his head, finally, and at first he hadn't believed the news, that vulgar little man

Jim Cott. But he'd read the writing on the wall and read it clearly; he'd come home when his time was up and then they'd chop him.

Yes, but he wouldn't lie down, he wouldn't indeed. They hadn't heard the last of Fenton Omerod. Disappointment had soured to bitterness, bitterness into anger, anger into a steady malice.

Just the same, he'd always been very careful. Those Germans, for instance—he'd handled them exquisitely. The approach had been beautifully made, not to the British Ambassador—that was unthinkable—but from one set of men of the world to another. For all his experience Fenton Omerod had been flattered but he'd still been extremely cautious. He had reason to be cautious for the proposal, as its outlines cleared, had been naked political dynamite. The country where Omerod served, they'd said, had enormous potential still untapped, a hardworking and still competitive people, a tradition of industrial growth. All it lacked today was capital, and it wouldn't get that from its major ally. Whereas if you looked a little west there was money running out of the banks. . . .

Fenton Omerod's first reaction had been simply to be scared. . . . Did they realize what they were saying? A whole province of this country had once spoken German, an excuse for acts which were better forgotten. And there was a Power which would hardly tolerate. . . .

Quite so, and we realize it perfectly. That is why we have come to you, to Sir Fenton Omerod, man of the world. ('We have, if we may remind you, Excellency, our own man here and perfectly competent.') But Sir Fenton would have the contacts too and could use them without the same suspicion —not the hardliners whose minds were closed, but the intelligent new men who were coming up, communists but not fanatics, the pragmatists, the patriots first.

It had been very well done for these Germans had been professionals; they'd never rushed it nor pressed him and he'd accepted them because they hadn't. Moreover they'd been gentlemen and to Fenton Omerod that was important. So he'd found them their contacts one by one, never moving from the impersonal shadows, feeling his way and theirs as

56

well, always correct and eternally cautious, above all things never Her Majesty's Ambassador. It had taken several weeks and he'd never heard the result of it, for they'd brought him home before it had ripened. He'd never heard the result of it, but like everyone else he'd heard the tanks.

All this was in his diaries now and he'd considered his book to its final end. Not that if he wrote this book a great many men would probably die: that wasn't the way Sir Fenton thought and in any case he'd disliked this people. But he'd considered very carefully what action they could take if he published; he'd even taken legal advice and an experienced lawyer had shrugged and smiled . . . Diaries? They weren't official papers, though of course if a fool wrote secrets in them he'd be asking for trouble and rightly receive it. No secrets? No *official* secrets? Yes, a delicate distinction. Inescapably he'd been British Ambassador, and whether an individual could divest himself of that splendid office, act as a private person and claim those rights. . . .

But he wasn't intending to publish the diaries, only the terrible story they held? The diaries would in fact be backing for what would otherwise just be ('Forgive me') journalism? That was rather a different cup of tea, from Omerod's point of view a sweeter. Of course if Omerod had been serving still it would blow his career to the moon and back, but it was evident he wasn't serving and if one wasn't being indiscreet he hadn't the aura of poverty. Pensions could be forfeited, though, in cases of what they called demerit, but that had been done extremely seldom and the lawyer gathered the risk was acceptable. Yes? Then I've said my piece.

Nevertheless he had hesitated. It wasn't his business but privately he was offended. He brought himself to say at last:

'Of course there's another aspect which will hardly have escaped you.'

'May I ask what it is?'

'You know what's just happened there. They're surviving in nominal freedom but only just. If you blow this story that won't last a day.'

'Is that another legal point?'

'I must accept the snub since I asked for it.' The eminent

lawyer picked up his hat. 'I think you know my fee but not where to send it. Send it to Oxfam.'

'Not to you?'

'No. Indeed no. Good morning, Sir Fenton.'

Omerod remembered this as he lay in bed. It hadn't even scratched his carapace. The nurse came in to put him to sleep and he looked at her, not hiding distaste. She was a West Indian woman, large and mumsy, and though he'd stuffily tried to shut her up she'd told him her story chattily. She hadn't intended to nurse again but her husband was out of work, there were seven to feed. She was fully trained and had first-class references, and the hospital had jumped at her when she'd gone to them and asked for work.

It would, Fenton thought. It was really disgraceful.

She tucked him up smiling comfortably, oblivious of his disapproval, giving him his sedative, turning the light out.

He woke in the small hours sluggishly, aware of something unusual but not of what. As his mind cleared he saw a man in the room, and as he finally came to consciousness he realized the man was masked. He reached for the bell but the man said softly:

'Pointless—the wire's cut.'

He put his hand out to the telephone.

'That too.'

Sir Fenton Omerod had started to sweat. 'There's no money here—no valuables either.'

'I haven't come for money or valuables.'

'Then what have you come for?' He'd spoken on an unthinking reflex.

'To show you something of what will happen if a book you're writing is ever published. Get out of bed.'

'I'm not supposed to yet, I—'

'Get out of bed.'

'My dressing gown—'

'God rot your dressing gown.'

Sir Fenton put his feet to the floor, feeling for his expensive slippers. They weren't by the bed and the floor felt cold. As he stood up the first blow caught him. It smashed the front teeth he was still rather proud of. He gasped and bent double and the man brought his knee up. This one broke Fenton

58

Omerod's nose but also it straightened him up again. He took a side-hand chop in the liver and fell to the floor. Through a pain which he'd never imagined he saw that the mumsy nurse had come in. She was standing there placidly, talking softly to the stranger.

'I didn't like him either,' she said, 'but I think you've done enough, man.'

'Who's going to stop me dishing out more?'

'I am,' she said, and he laughed at her.

From a distinctly mumsy bosom the mumsy nurse produced a razor. She flicked it open expertly and stood holding it lightly, practised. 'I know just what you're thinking—I'm a woman and you could take me. Sure enough. But I'll mark you before you get me and I'll mark you so your wife won't know you.'

It was what he feared worse than a bullet in the belly, the scars of a razor-brawl, the ridicule of professional friends. He stood watching her silently, undecided.

'What now, man? Make up your mind.'

He looked down at Fenton Omerod who seemed to be unconscious now. 'Okay,' he said. 'So he's had enough.'

'Then put him back on the bed again. Don't make a noise.'

He put Sir Fenton back on the bed.

'And now, man, beat it. There's a window outside in the corridor.'

'I didn't come through the window.'

'I don't care how you came, that's how you're going.'

She stood back two paces to let him pass, watching his movements carefully. She still had the cut-throat, its edge pointing upwards, as she followed him into the corridor. He put his legs across the windowsill, hanging by his hands, the knuckles white.

'It's the hell of a drop.'

'Man, you're getting paid for it.'

He hung still, a little scared.

The nurse slashed at his knuckles suddenly, first at one hand, then the other. The gesture had been almost playful—this wasn't a serious cutting. She heard him gasp with the pain of it, then the hands disappeared and she heard the fall.

She looked out of the window unhurriedly. He was limping towards a car in the shadows, his hands in his jacket pockets, pressed to his sides.

She went back to the private room and Fenton Omerod. She hadn't been lying, her papers were genuine. She was a professional nurse with professional standards and she ran over Fenton Omerod thoroughly. His pulse was a flutter, his breathing shallow. This snobbish old man was shocked but would probably live.

She went out again to the corridor, walking to the end of it. There was a telephone there and she rang to the duty doctor. That was her nurse's duty and she did it.

The hospital never saw her again.

CHAPTER SEVEN

Russell and Julia Hartley were received by the hospital Registrar, his manner a delicate blend of regret and resentment. The regret was explicit and wholly genuine : a patient in his hospital had suffered further injury and a good doctor's conscience was outraged bitterly. Sir Fenton now had a broken nose and he'd lost some teeth he was still very proud of; he'd had a blow where a man of his age should not, but though he'd been severely shocked an X-ray had shown no permanent damage. They could see him if they wished to but there was little point in doing so. Naturally he was sedated heavily. Tomorrow for ten minutes, perhaps?

So the sympathy had been simply expressed but the resentment rather more subtly. Nevertheless they had read it clearly. An incident of this shocking kind was unheard of in any well-run hospital, and though the Registrar didn't put it in terms he conveyed his impression perfectly that a patient who attracted one was a patient to be got rid of firmly. Mrs Hartley had asked when her father could leave? At his daughter's convenience. Medically speaking, say ten days or a fortnight. Any aftercare necessary would of course be arranged. The Registrar was a doctor and he proposed to stay within doctor's limits. There was however a Superintendent of Police who was very anxious to talk to them. The Registrar had given him a room along the corridor. Till tomorrow then, and accept my sympathy.

It was in fact a Chief Superintendent and he rose as they came in to him. Russell had never met him but it was obvious that he recognized Russell. He said at once :

'May I ask if you're in this officially, sir ?'

'No, I am not. You could call me a friend of the family, of Mrs Hartley in particular, and she happened to be with me when the message from the hospital came through. Naturally I motored her here.'

The Superintendent was a self-confident man but for a moment he looked uncertain. Since Russell was there he would have liked to talk freely, but with a woman he didn't know he was much less sure. Russell read his thought promptly.

'I should explain that my friendship with Mrs Hartley stems from her having worked for me.'

'Is that so ?' The Superintendent looked relieved at once, turning to Julia, reassured. 'Then I'd better tell you what we've discovered, though it doesn't make much of a picture if you regard it as simply police work. A man broke in here last night and attacked your father. Sir Fenton babbled before they sedated him but it wasn't very helpful. Something about some diaries.' He looked at Julia Hartley inquiringly.

'As you say,' she said levelly, 'that's not very helpful.'

The Superintendent smiled politely, suspecting there was a story here, equally certain it wasn't for him. 'The rest of the tale is still pretty blurred. A masked man whom your father of course didn't recognize broke in and began to beat him up, but a West Indian nurse arrived and stopped him. Your father was injured and only half conscious but he thought he saw her draw a razor. That bit does fit since there's blood on an outside windowsill. It isn't Sir Fenton's group nor yet the nurse's. We know because they group them as possible donors when they arrive.' The Superintendent looked at Russell, a question forming, clearly an awkward one.

Russell spared him the asking. 'She wasn't one of ours, if

you're wondering that. You'll realize I'd tell you at once if she were.'

'I accept that, sir—thank you. Moreover she's disappeared, which won't surprise you. They took her on on references and she seems to have been a genuine nurse. Rather a good one, the doctors tell me.'

'You'll try to trace her, naturally.'

'Of course, but it doesn't look hopeful. It's significant that she went at once. She wasn't a woman to run in fright and her conduct, if Sir Fenton is right, was hardly that of a thief's accomplice. So if she wasn't working for you she had other masters, who will have got her out of the country by now, and her family too if she really had one. That we *can* check and I'll bet against it.'

'Police work—' Charles Russell began.

'You read my mind. There's been an assault on a well-to-do patient in a hospital. *Prima facie* motive robbery. Talking to you, sir, I've private doubts, but I work for a Chief Constable, not in Whitehall.'

'You put it very prettily.'

'I'm delighted we understand each other. And talking of police work I've put a constable in the room with him. He's there to take a statement when Sir Fenton comes out of his sedative, but I don't think I need tell you that he also has other instructions. There'll be no second assault on Sir Fenton Omerod.' The Chief Superintedent waved a hand. 'Police protection is mostly terrible eyewash, but when you've got a man immobile, tucked up in bed and can't get up, a local man is just as effective as, well, say a sharper-trained one.'

'He is indeed.'

'But I hope that you'll keep us in touch, sir. We don't want to know what we shouldn't know—quite to the contrary. Unnecessary knowledge is always an embarrassment. But if any, er, organization should take a further interest in this affair we should wish to know. You realize much better than I do how these things can go off the rails if we're kept in the dark.'

'I've never done that and I never shall.'

'I know, sir—that's why I'm talking.' He shook hands with

them quickly. 'Beatings-up in hospital, diaries, black nurses who disappear. . . . I'm a policeman and proud to be one. And always at your service, of course. If you don't find me here the station can contact me.'

'You're very kind.'

'Not kind at all but I try to be co-operative.'

They went down to the hospital courtyard and Russell's new car. It was a two-eighty Mercedes coupé and he hadn't bought it as a folly with his gratuity on retirement. He wasn't a rich man but nor was he poor, and he could have afforded a Mercedes at almost any time he had considered one. The fact remained he never had. So long as he'd been serving, the ageing prestigious Humber had suited his background perfectly, antiquated but not quite an antique. But now the Executive lay behind him the monstrous old chariot was the mark of the beast, and Charles Russell in retirement had no wish to be labelled Grand Old Man. So he had bought the Mercedes and drove it beautifully, with all of his forty years' experience but with something too of a young man's panache. He handed Julia Hartley in.

'Where do we go from here?' she asked him.

'For luncheon?'

'I didn't mean that.'

'I didn't really think you did.'

He drove confidently away from the hospital, for he knew this country perfectly, the enchanting lanes still hidden between the roaring highways. He pulled into a gate and waited.

'So Lissdale meant business,' she said at last. 'He was telling me as much as he knew. I can guess who ordered the beating-up so it follows they beat my father to scare him, to frighten him off that book of his. Then Lissdale's side took a hand as he said and they seem to have stopped the worst of it.'

He nodded, relieved, for he hated to have to spell it out. 'And Satra's little misfortune at Guildford was anything but what it seemed.' Russell laughed but without amusement. 'They're pretty efficient, they always were, especially when it's a question of time.'

'Do we tell Josef Satra what really happened?'

'Did you tell him Lord Lissdale picked you up?'

She shook her head.

'Then I don't see any advantage—none. But there's something I must know from you. Do you think that attack will work as they meant, scare your father into calling that book of his back from Vane?'

'It's hard to say. I don't think he's a courageous man, or not in the sense that he'd stand much violence, but he's stubborn as hell and still resilient.'

'You could add your own persuasions to the gentleman's who beat him up.'

'I can't do that, you know I can't. His daughter of all people.'

'I understand.'

'But I'll confess I'd very much like to. And I've cheated a bit already when I asked you to the house. I said I wanted you to cool him off lest the book fall flat and disappoint him, but really I wanted the whole thing dropped. I always did and now more than ever. The more we suspect, the more that develops, the more that book frightens me. And not only for my father, either. If the people it's going to damage have been trying to frighten my father off, then I can't entirely blame them.'

'I understand,' he said again.

'You're a wonderfully understanding man.'

Charles Russell produced two bottles of lager, two glasses and a bottle-opener. He had always been careful of details when they mattered. 'It won't be as cold as it should be,' he told her.

She drank her lager and Russell watched her. . . . A most competent woman and still a woman. Maybe if he'd been twenty years younger. . . . He checked himself for this was idle. But you could put your cards down on the table and she'd match them as you played them out.

'There was another side to Lissdale's message.' His voice was as cool as the lager wasn't.

'The implication that they were warning you off?'

He spread his hands on the wheel and she heard him chuckle. 'Implication is right—it wasn't explicit. But it's happened before, it's the way they play it. Perfectly sensible too

—no third parties. I can recognize what's familiar enough.'

'If you're telling me that you want to drop out—'

He looked at her, for a moment affronted, then decided he'd put it ambiguously. 'They haven't exactly frightened me as the other side tried to frighten your father, but they've made me think, which they meant to do, which inhibits any official action.'

'I don't follow that.'

'Use your head—you've a good one. Your father's quite safe for several days, but suppose I took this story to the Executive. Your father's not out in the clear, far from it; he's intending something damaging—damaging to this state as well. You can't guarantee that they'd see it as you do, as a personal problem affecting your father. They might take a very different view, and though I could put them in gear if I wanted I couldn't in any way limit their action.'

She thought this over for several minutes. 'Some action awkward for father?' she asked.

He hesitated but finally said it. 'Your father's a bit of a bastard, you know.'

'If he is my father.' It came out savagely.

'I didn't mean that though of course I've heard gossip.'

'Perhaps you didn't, Charles, but I did. I meant just that and in some ways I'm pleased.'

'Anyway, you're a marvellous daughter.'

'Oh no, I'm not—by God I'm not. I'm a woman in a corner and I don't know any way out of it. I've accepted his name, his protection when I was growing up. I've something to repay and I'm beholden to repay it.'

'I understand that too. I'm in debt myself.'

'What on earth can you mean?'

He didn't answer her directly. 'I told you it could be dangerous to tell this story to the Executive. They'd be obliged to take it to Harry Tuke, and if Tuke took the view which he very well might—'

'My father—' she said.

'Would certainly be a principal in a drama which might develop in several ways. Let's leave it at that.' He smiled almost shyly. 'But for the little I'm worth myself I'm at your service.'

At first she looked unbelieving. 'You'd come into this personally knowing where it could lead to? You'd do that to pay for the snippets I once passed on to you?'

Characteristically he ducked it. 'Good heavens no, nothing so reputable. Just say I'm a sucker for women and always have been. Pretty women, that it.'

This time she laughed; she understood him very well. Charles Russell would go to the stake and worse before admitting a motive which did him credit. So she laughed and dismissed it, but for once she wasn't entirely right. She understood Russell very well but she didn't quite know him perfectly. He'd been thinking about late middle age, the years which a generous God and good health now offered. They could be fruitful years before death knocked, or a sterile barren delay before the cold. It all depended on how you handled them. It was absurd, no doubt, to pretend to be young : after thirty years of desk work it would be ludicrous to start waving guns. Charles Russell didn't intend to. What he intended was a calculated avoidance, the avoidance of too much discipline and of over-rigid habits. At sixty one wasn't elastic still, one had one's little drills for things and was fully entitled to do so. They made life simpler, they spun out leisure, but what was very dangerous was when the drill became its own reward, not the muddle avoided, the moment saved, but the deadly satisfaction of having completed some trifle efficiently. If that was the trap of old age, its threshold, then Russell had seen it and wouldn't step over. Clichés were mostly right, he thought, so variety was the spice of life, and thinking in clichés one might as well hammer the nail in hard. There was life in the old dog yet, there really was. All you need do was to watch the spark.

Russell started to talk again, almost gaily. 'So instead of going to the Executive, who would certainly have to report to Tuke, I'll talk to Harry Tuke myself. We're still pretty close.'

'That would help?'

'Not directly. But to some extent it would cover us and in this game that's very important.'

A considerable woman, she hid disappointment, but in

66

fact it was unfounded. Russell was going on quickly, he'd done his thinking.

'And there's another thing we must do at once. We must get those diaries and put them where they're really safe.' He didn't allow her time to protest nor believe she'd consider doing so. 'In a safe in a country house they're absurdly vulnerable. Do you know the combination?'

'There's some jewellery which belongs to me. Nothing much but I keep it there.'

'So much the better. The fewer people on this excursion and the happier I shall be. I've peculiar friends still and some of them are highly skilled, but I didn't want to bring one unless I had to. Now I don't.'

'But you'll be taking me?'

'If you want to come.'

'It's father's house. I think I'd better.'

He put the car in gear and began to move. 'At midnight, then. I'll call for you.'

'You could make it earlier. I had a dinner engagement tonight but I'm going to call off.'

There was something in her tone which caught his ear. As he changed up smoothly he asked her as gently: 'May I ask with whom?'

'With Josef Satra.'

'Keep it,' Charles Russell said. 'You must certainly keep it.'

'Charles, you must be joking. Satra's people attacked my father—'

'He knew nothing about it, I'm sure of that.'

'How can you be sure?'

'From thirty years' experience. He doesn't do that sort of work and there's a principle called the Need To Know which they follow very rigidly. You can take it from me he knew nothing of this.'

'Just the same it was his people.'

'Just the same he's a contact and it's foolish to cut them.'

'I'm going to find it difficult. Will this business of father find its way to the evening newspapers?'

He shrugged. 'A paragraph—it's hardly world-shaking.'

'So if he didn't know what's happened before, he could know when I go to meet him?'

'Yes.'

'And you still expect me to dine with him?' She looked at him fiercely. 'Is that an order?'

'I never give silly orders.'

'I'll go.'

His Excellency the Ambassador pushed the paper away with a sour distaste. It was a memorandum from Josef Satra, written in terms of protest, even of outrage, and His Excellency was justifiably angry. For one thing it was no part of a Military Attaché's duties to query, and in writing, an operation which didn't concern him; and for another the language was immoderate, disrespectful. These were serious matters, breaches of protocol, though the Ambassador wasn't a man to lean on protocol heavily. What disturbed him was less the words than the writer's motive. Satra had seen the evening paper, and Fenton Omerod had been beaten up; Satra hadn't a very agile mind but for this one he'd hardly needed it and he'd put two and two together correctly, something he was quite free to do as long as he kept his mouth shut. But he hadn't, he'd dashed off a scalding memo, and the memo had put the Ambassador on the horns.

He had known he was already on them, but this had increased their sharpness, the immediate thrust. He had already reported home that Josef Satra had been in the West too long; it had already been more than half suggested that he was somehow trying to shield the man. Though this hadn't been formally true it had made him wince, for in his way he had rather admired Josef Satra and was reluctant to break him casually. The boy had picked up some strange ideas, preposterous Western fallacies about liberalizing a tried regime, but his loyalty, up to now at least, had never been in question once. He was a good Party man still, above all things a patriot.

All this had counted heavily but it no longer outweighed this disgraceful memo. Going on about violence, a minimal violence. As though Fenton Omerod's person mattered, as though his life were important—any life. This was heresy and therefore serious. The Ambassador saw that he'd made a mistake : Josef Satra was worse than tainted, he'd gone soft. The West had got him for this was its language. Moral judgment and words like unlawful. Ach! His Excellency sought for the phrase and found it. It was the worst in his book but he feared it fitted. These were the words of liberal humanism. The boy was totally useless now and that must be reported clearly.

He rang the bell and sent for Satra.

Who came in at once in a blazing rage, but he had it under a soldier's control, and the Ambassador could recognize that. Some shreds of his old respect came back but not enough to change his decision.

'Sit down,' he said curtly.

Satra sat.

His Excellency tapped the memo. 'You realize this is an outrage, of course.'

'I realize it is irregular—very. I deny the views are outrageous at all.'

'I don't see how you can hold to that. You know perfectly what's at stake, I think.'

'Of course I know perfectly what's at stake.'

The Ambassador said dangerously : 'If I'm reading this paper correctly then you seem to be trying to tell me that the end doesn't always justify the means.'

'You'll realize that's an abstraction, sir, but it isn't one which I'd always dissent from.'

. . . He'll have to go home, he really will. Perhaps they can manage to save him still but they'll have to start the job from scratch.

'Then leaving abstractions aside as we should, will you tell me, please, what you find to object to?'

'Violence. Uncivilized violence.'

'Uncivilized? Whose civilization?'

Josef Satra didn't answer him and His Excellency considered it. It was every bit as bad as he'd feared but another thought crossed his mind like a shadow and the hard old man was also just. 'The man who was beaten-up was Sir Fenton Omerod. I think I hinted once before that I knew about your relationship with his daughter.'

'Now ended for ever. Brutally.'

The Ambassador gasped. This was a further and deadly symptom of decadence, this putting a personal feeling, sex at that, before an established principle, public duty. The man was really rotten right through.

But Josef Satra was talking again, almost, the Ambassador thought, to himself. 'I was going to give her dinner tonight. Now she won't come.'

'She's telephoned to excuse herself?'

'No.'

His Excellency smiled frostily. 'Then take an older man's advice. Keep your appointment, your friend will be there. Englishwomen of that class don't simply stand their men up. That would be inconsiderate, therefore rude. If she hasn't called off expressly then she'll be there. Believe me, I know. I was in this country before when I was young. It hasn't much changed in many ways. I *know*.'

Satra stayed silent and now the Ambassador failed to read him. He said testily :

'Don't stare like an owl, man. If you've anything more to say I'll listen.'

'You haven't a clue what drives me, have you?'

'To write that ridiculous memo? Yes, I have.'

'Your Excellency is for once mistaken.'

'Then give it a name and leave me to think.'

'I wrote that paper in desperate fear.'

'For yourself? It was hardly helpful.'

'Not for myself, for Julia Hartley.'

There was a pencil between the Ambassador's fingers and suddenly there were two pieces of pencil. He was grey, he looked ninety. 'You feared some mischief to Julia Hartley?'

'Why not? I know the form. You fail with a man so you switch to the woman. It's all in the book, I've read it too.'

'You must be insane.'

'Perhaps. But I'm not quite ignorant.'

His Excellency pulled himself upright heavily. The greyness had gone, he was dangerously flushed. 'Get out of my sight, you rat,' he said.

'As Your Excellency pleases.'

'Get out, get out, get out.'

70

When Satra had gone the Ambassador shivered. It had simply never occurred to him. No, but the thought had occurred to Satra, which meant it might well occur to others. The next orders he got might indeed be just those.

He poured himself an enormous whisky. . . . Julia, Julia Omerod-Hartley. . . .

He had very good reasons for wishing no ill to her.

It was unusual for Lord Lissdale to be meeting his chief contact in person. He liked to think of him as his principal contact but in fact he pulled the strings which danced him. Lord Lissdale's own estimate of where he stood in the hierarchy was a very sour joke with the men who controlled him. They thought of him as another agent, one specially useful within his limits, but no more the stuff to inherit power than were the men Lord Lissdale himself despised. It was seldom worth risking a meeting directly, he had the usual arrangements for drops and timed calls, but when the matter was urgent the risk was accepted. And this matter was urgent and something more.

Lissdale's contact was saying sharply : 'Well?' His instincts were much more urbane than his manner but included the depressing certainty that if you gave Lord Lissdale an inch he would take an ell. With agents that was always disastrous. This formidable but civilized man had little respect for English hirelings and his manner with them was always severe, the impression he sought increased by his barber. He had stiff and exceptionally thick black hair and he wore it cut down in a ruthless crewcut. It was ugly and it was meant to be. Lissdale thought of him as Crophead which he wouldn't have resented : on the contrary he'd have been gratified since a protective shell of near brutality was part of the aura he'd built up deliberately. So he said again harshly : 'Well?'

'It's got into the evening paper, but naturally not the background. The nurse was one of ours, I take it.'

'Of course she was.'

'And Mrs Hartley did go straight to Russell. She was with him when the hospital called so he motored her there as a matter of course.'

'So far so good, that's all as I planned.'

'Then why have you sent for me?'

'Because you've got another job.' Crophead considered. He wished to tell Lissdale no more than he need but he realized he would be useless blind. 'You know we've had their codes for weeks and behind this book stand Omerod's diaries. Without them the book could be silly gossip but with them it's a powerful weapon. A weapon in our hands, not theirs.'

'I've heard rumours of diaries myself, you know.'

'For once they were right.' Crophead tapped the table thoughtfully. His hands belied the ugly crewcut, sensitive hands and beautifully kept. 'Do you think,' he asked suddenly, 'this beating will really influence Omerod?'

'It's early days to tell but it might. I wouldn't call Fenton Omerod hero.'

'He could call the book off?'

'It's possible.'

'Then we've got to have those diaries ourselves, publish them as they stand if necessary.'

Lord Lissdale nodded. 'Logical.'

'Where do you think they are? With his publisher?'

'They're the backing to the book, not the book itself.'

'At his bank?'

'I don't know.'

'Is there a safe in Omerod's house?'

'There usually is in that sort of place.'

'Then we'd better have a look at it. Tonight. I'll send a man with you who knows his trade but naturally you will go with him. He'll call for you this evening and you'll be ready.'

CHAPTER EIGHT

Sir Albert Bull was thinking it over dourly for it wasn't the first time events had mistimed themselves. He had been to see Fenton Omerod and had left him with much the worst of it. That hadn't been remarkable since he, Albert Bull, had held a very poor hand. Now it was a notably better but also rather too late to play it. It was notably better because His Excellency the Ambassador had just been round to see him urgently, and His Excellency had spoken freely, barely hiding what was a naked appeal. Fenton Omerod had been keeping diaries and those diaries, standing behind his book, could tear the Ambassador's country to pieces. The Ambassador didn't want that and nor would Bull. After all, Fenton Omerod had been one of his people. His Excellency had been frank, he hadn't shuffled; he'd told as much of the truth as he dared and no lies whatever. That made him, in Bull's opinion, an excellent diplomat. He was the sort of man you could deal with, not like the French, and Albert Bull's instinct as well as his professional interest was to help this unhappy country if he could find a way to do so.

. . . Diaries—a deplorable habit. It was dubious in most people since a substitute for real experience, and in officials of whatever rank diaries were clearly the work of the devil. Sir Albert Bull sighed. If he'd known about these diaries when he'd been down to Omerod's hospital he'd have known perfectly well how to handle his weapon. . . . But they were private diaries, entirely personal? But of course. Nobody was suggesting that a man of Fenton Omerod's experience would consider an open breach of an Act, but there were shades and degrees of secrecy, and the higher one climbed the ladder the more delicate the distinctions became. That was agreed by all men of good sense. And had Her Majesty's Ambassador the right to a private record at all? Was it practical to distinguish here, the man from the high official? Fenton Omerod would no doubt have answered and Bull would have conceded nothing, but without this new weapon he now held too late he had had to appeal to personal feeling, the traditions of the Service which he personally thought were in any case ridiculous. There were rules about writing books in retirement, but they hadn't many teeth nor sharp ones. But diaries were very different. Bull sighed again unhappily. If he'd known about these diaries he could have used a discreet but effective stick. He wouldn't have threatened nor even have felt the need to do so, since he was far too good a diplomatist to paint himself into a corner with overt threats. But the menace would have been there all right, the more effective for not being stated.

And now he couldn't use it—somebody else had. A different sort of threat and more effective. Violence. Do not publish your book or this will happen again, this and much more, much more and worse. Though that wasn't the story from Omerod's hospital, where the official line was as clear as mud : someone had broken in to rob a presumably wealthy private patient and, disturbed in intended robbery, had lost his head and attacked his victim. Sir Albert Bull grinned. He didn't credit a word of it for he didn't believe in coincidence, especially when it didn't fit. There'd been excellent motive to frighten Omerod and the people who had that motive were known. Their representative in this country had just been talking to Albert Bull. . . . Had His Excellency approved the attack, had His Excellency even known of it? Perhaps he had and perhaps he had not. In that sort of embassy all was possible, the real power held by some faceless junior. On the whole Bull thought the Ambassador had been privy, but it wasn't the sort of question one asked him. His Excellency hadn't ignored it, though : that would have been clumsy, even suspicious. Instead he'd blandly accepted the published story, expressing his formal regrets as *cher collègue*. It was really most deplorable and Sir Albert would please convey his condolences.

Sir Albert had said he would but he didn't intend to. He'd never liked Fenton Omerod—now he loathed him. Those diaries would prove nothing legally, but inevitably they'd be circumstantial, they'd be more than enough to support a book; they could blow an innocent country to shreds and label their author as wholly untrustworthy.

Sir Albert Bull scowled since he didn't wish either, but he had something more to worry him than the fate of a country he'd never seen or world opinion to savage his own. Like Russell he'd had vast experience, different but as comprehensive, and like Russell he'd smelt the political essence : if somebody wanted that book suppressed there'd be somebody else who wanted it published. They'd want that very badly indeed and they were powerful enough to get what they wanted.

. . . Those diaries again, those goddamned diaries. This was certainly a matter for the highest grade of Security, but the question was which that was and how to reach it. British security, like American and more so Russian, was a jungle of overlapping empires, or if that sounded too like official jargon you could simply call it a shocking mess. It wasn't so bad as the French perhaps, a world of parallel police— enchanting phrase—of riot squads and internal scandal. But it was a mess just the same and one had to walk warily.

It was a thousand pities that Bull's predecessor had been so stupid, effectively blocking the lines to the Security Executive. He had detested Charles Russell for the most futile of reasons, holding that all ex-soldiers were useless, Russell's particular brand of soldier so dim as to be actively dangerous. It wasn't a view which Albert Bull shared, and though Russell was now an *éminence grise* his successor was quietly shaking down. There were fences to be mended here and Albert Bull intended to mend them. For the moment he'd been too busy in this rat-ridden stable they'd asked him to clean, but a working peace with the Security Executive was high on his list of priorities. Just for the present he didn't have it, certainly not the understanding which would engage the fruitful interest of a body of men which he couldn't command. Only Tuke and the Prime Minister could deal directly with the Executive, and Bull couldn't go to either without telling his own Minister first. And the less said of that one the soonest mended. If you told him this story he'd start preaching at once.

Which left Albert Bull with a bad second best, those people down at Fifty-five, those peasants from Fifty-five, God help him.

He considered it very carefully since Fifty-five were not the Executive. They had an aura all their own which Bull mistrusted, the minor public school gentility plus a streak of too often unreasonable violence. They had had their successes but their failures had been more numerous. The Executive had on occasion failed too, but when it failed it failed in silence. When Fifty-five stumbled it cracked the pavement, and publicly, for all to see. They were efficient perhaps, but they weren't adroit. But Albert Bull was in a corner. He picked up a telephone, then put it down again; he shrugged but he finally made his call.

The man who was shown in ten minutes later was if anything worse than Bull had feared. As he hung up his bowler hat he said:

'Willy's on leave so I got your call. I'm keeping his chair warm till Monday week.'

'Willy?'

'Baron Cosh of Bexhill.'

'I see.'

It didn't offend Sir Albert Bull that Lord Cosh had a name which made Whitehall snigger, far less that that worthy maid of all work should be honoured with a discreet life peerage. There'd been others, Bull thought, a great deal stranger. What worried him was to hear him called Willy. The boss should never be Willy—never.

'I hope you don't mind that I'm here instead.'

'I sometimes take leave myself, you know.'

'So what can we do for you?'

Bull inspected his visitor shrewdly. He wore a dapper blue suit, a hard white collar, and a tie which Bull thought he recognized. When he looked again he realized he didn't. The resemblance was remarkable and very probably deliberate, but the difference was there when you looked for it, just sufficient to excuse the wearer if somebody openly challenged him. There was also a large moustache and a candid smile, a carefully studied impression of the ex-pilot. Bull thought of such men as a class, not as persons, and privately he called them 'It'. He began *pianissimo*.

'This is a little delicate.'

'Of course,' It said.

Sir Albert Bull felt his experienced way. 'It's a matter of an ex-diplomatist's diaries, Sir Fenton Omerod's deplorable diaries. You know where he was last *en poste*?'

It shook his head and Sir Albert told him.

'Aha!'

'Aha again, whatever that means.' Bull had thought of adding 'my man' but had not. He detested the bogus Service type, but he was courteous and he needed help. Just the same It was pulling his nerves to pieces. 'Those diaries could cause us a great deal of trouble. There'd be disaster in the country which almost certainly they're concerned with, and naturally we'd be blamed for the leak.'

'Where are these diaries?'

'I don't know that. In a bank, I hope.'

'Then I don't think we can help you. Doing banks is beyond us normally.'

Sir Albert stared blankly, seriously considering an end to the conversation there and then. If this was how these men were taught to think. . . . He collected himself but his voice was acid. 'I don't think you're quite following me. I don't want these diaries, very far from it, but I'm afraid that somebody else does badly. If they're now in Sir Fenton Omerod's bank there may still be means to deal with his book, but if they fall into hands I'm thinking of we're in very serious trouble indeed.'

'I do follow that much.'

. . . And high time too.

'In a bank, as you hinted, they're pretty safe, but if he's keeping them in his private house—'

'Easy. We'll get them.'

Sir Albert exploded. 'You will, my friend, do no such thing. Now listen and listen carefully. You could oblige us in this matter and in Lord Cosh's regretted absence I hope you will. But the service will be limited and I'm now limiting it specifically. If you wish to decline the commission, do so.'

'Shoot it.'

. . . Oh God.

'I want you to keep an eye on Omerod's house. You're not to break in, far less blow his safe, but nor is anyone else to. You watch and that's all. That's all, that is, unless somebody else tries to do what I fear. In that case I must concede you discretion.'

It nodded knowingly, scaring Bull. 'Understood but it sounds too subtle to me. Wouldn't it be much simpler—?'

'No, it would not.'

'If you say so, of course.'

'I say so unequivocally.' Sir Albert Bull rose. 'You accept the commission, the job if you prefer it?'

'Willco,' It said. 'Roger and Out.'

This time Sir Albert's stare was a gape. He hadn't believed his ears but the man had said it.

Julia Hartley took a taxi down to Prunier's again in a mood which she would have described herself as more than a little edgy. For one thing she wouldn't have gone at all if Charles Russell hadn't pressed her to, and for another the evening post had come in with a second and troubling letter from Kendal Hartley. It had made her fume quietly for it had been quintessential Kendal. He had written before that he wasn't quite happy. His university was researching on some project for the military, and though it seemed harmless he hadn't been sure. Now he was sure and he didn't like it; he was thinking of resigning and coming home.

His wife frowned uneasily. That was Kendal at his maddening worst, and she had a healthy female contempt for too-tender conscience. It was all very well to write learnedly of *Sturm und Drang*, of the spiritual tensions which distracted the intellectual. A woman had to live with them and might see them less romantically; she might even, in a sleepless night, look at them with a dangerous realism, a man's knowledge or at least belief that his talents were above the normal, his ignorance or self-saving blindness to the fact that he lacked the strength to apply them. Naturally such a man felt frustrated, naturally he suffered his *angst*. A suspiciously woolly Teutonic word, but whatever you called it the man felt thwarted. Let him simmer in that for a while and you had it, the disease in full flower, the classic symptoms—if it makes money it can't be honest, if it's successful it can't be good. It was very hard indeed to live with and harder still to effect a cure. It was in fact impossible if there was anything like a spark of love left. For you couldn't tell Kendal the truth, he couldn't take it. He'd accepted a post in an American university, and he wasn't an insular man nor ignorant. So what did he think the Americans were? Why shouldn't they use the brains which they'd hired? If a child thought like this you would try to explain, but Kendal Hartley would smile politely, hiding his conviction that you were a materialist and a barbarian.

As she went into Prunier's Satra rose and Julia's private spirits rose with him. He wasn't civilized in Kendal's sense and certainly he wasn't as clever, but he had something important which Kendal lacked and Julia had a need of it.

She'd been wondering how he'd start the ball and he left her in no doubt of it. He said over drinks with an utter candour, the more effective since clearly he hadn't considered his words :

'I didn't expect you to come, you know.'

She knew what he meant but she wasn't quite ready, standing him off as her instinct dictated. 'Because you couldn't make it before? But you sounded pretty shaken when you rang.'

'Not too shaken but ashamed.'

. . . If he knew who'd picked me up that night, that he'd warned me and Charles Russell too. . . .

Clearly he didn't, his shame was genuine. 'I fell into the silliest trap. I was knocked out cold and robbed like a baby.'

'I want to hear the details,' she said. She still wasn't ready for what was coming.

He told her quickly, sorely embarrassed. A man like Satra would be, she thought; he'd feel this as humiliation, a personal and a bitter one.

'You've told the police of course,' she said.

'No, I have not, I'd rather take it. I had a few pounds but it might have been more, and my watch was hardly worth the stealing. But I'm sorry about my cigarette case. That was my father's; I valued it greatly.' He looked at her, still grimly humourless. 'Besides,' he said, 'there's a sort of convention. Diplomats who go to the police are not exactly popular with their seniors. That sort of publicity. . . .'

He was thinking he'd something more than a hunch that his stock had already fallen severely, but he left the sentence unfinished and started again. 'No, that wasn't the reason I thought you'd not come.'

She'd have to face it sooner or later. 'Since you put it like that I nearly didn't.'

'I'd like to know the truth at once. I read about your father in a newspaper and quite by chance. That was the first I knew of it. I'd like you to believe that, please, though I don't suppose you ever will.'

'Why shouldn't I believe it, please?'

'I'd rather you didn't fence with me. You know about your father's book, you know what that book could do and where. I'm a man of that country and proud to be one.'

She almost laughed but managed not to. It was very unsophisticated: Kendal Hartley would never talk like that, but then Satra wasn't an intellectual. It was one of the things she found exciting.

There were others, she knew as they went to their table. He was solid and male, somehow shy but assured. The trouble was the man was serious. If he'd suggested a liaison she might very well have gone to him, but she'd never have to decide since he'd never ask. God damn the male beast, the beast was serious.

She asked because she wanted to know: 'You talked of trouble in your country if my father does bring that book out. What sort of trouble and what would break?'

'The roof would fall in for good and all. I've seen it written in your newspapers that those others came in for military reasons, some talk of the western frontier threatened. I think that's much too glib and slick. Politics still rule them in the pinches where it matters, so since they came in they came for politics.'

'But you don't know what politics?'

'A lot of my friends are guessing,' he said. He was cautious and she didn't resent it.

'And you think that my father may know the real reason?'

'It's possible he's got it right, but I don't think the truth really matters that much. I think they came in on suspicion, you see, an instinct that we were going too far. In that case any reason would do, any credible reason to justify action. It wouldn't have to be true, just look convincing. And then they could say "I told you so", and bang would come down the shutters for ever.'

'I don't want my father to do that either.'

'I know you don't, I believe you sincerely.' He drank some wine without seeming to taste it, then said suddenly as an open challenge: 'It's a very good country. I love it deeply.'

'I'd like to visit it again one day.'

'You can come when you like, for your life if you wish it. Tomorrow, I'd say, if I thought I dared to.'

She dropped her eyes for it wasn't on. He mightn't always be a diplomatist, which meant service in garrison towns, an alien. She'd be part of a Vatican-rigid hierarchy, talking to other soldiers' wives, to the women of Party members on an equal or similar rung of the ladder. Bearing his children, bringing them up. Bringing up children in a language you didn't dream in. No. And she'd never be really trusted. No indeed.

But he was saying in his quiet strong voice: 'What do you plan to do for your father?'

She answered the question literally. 'Take him out just as soon as he's fit to leave, then I'll bring him home and arrange a good nurse.' Now she looked up again. 'Also a man to take very good care of him.'

'That would be very wise,' he said. He said it without a tremor of guilt, as a matter of simple practical fact. Josef Satra would have been much surprised if he'd known what emotion he'd roused in Julia. Not for the first time she wholly admired him. She admired his commitment, it made life simpler. It could also make it a little eerie.

'I won't have him beaten again,' she said.

'I could suggest a guarantee of that. You could bring him to my country with you. I don't think he'd publish his book if he saw us now, and we're a hospitable and an ancient people.'

. . . He's trying again and it's still not on. It was out of the question, hopelessly out. And her birth—these things followed you. Josef Satra wouldn't care about that; he was a man in love and fighting hard, but this hospitable and ancient people had traditions which hadn't been bent with the wind. Since you mustn't now call them bourgeois you could only call them Victorian. Madame Satra, a foreigner —that would be bad. But that English wife of the Major Satra, some story which clung to her skirts still, unproven— that would be double death for them both.

She looked at her watch : it was somehow eleven. 'I ought to get some sleep,' she said.

He paid the bill and found her a taxi. As he handed her in she said softly, astonishing herself :

'I could give you a drink if you feel you'd like one.'

She saw him freeze but he managed a smile. 'But a drink,' he said, 'is not what I want.'

Three persons were on the line that evening, checking a matter of common interest. The first was Julia Hartley herself, who rang to Charles Russell at a quarter to midnight. . . . Yes, he was ready and glad that she was. He'd be round at her flat in ten minutes precisely.

The second was a nameless man, the man whom Crophead had said knew his trade. He rang Lord Lissdale from a call box and he didn't trust people with titles at all. His Lordship, he asked acidly, was prepared for a certain job as arranged? He was? He had better be.

The third was Sir Albert Bull from the Office. He often stayed late since he often had to. He rang to confirm with Fifty-five. . . . The matter they had discussed was now in hand? From this evening? Excellent. So everything was under control?

Yes, everything was under control.

The words were belied in a matter of hours as the wildest exaggeration.

CHAPTER NINE

Charles Russell and Julia Hartley were driving in Russell's car to Surrey. Julia was on edge again but Russell seemed as relaxed as ever, driving fast but without a hint of risk, humming an air which Julia knew. Occasionally there was a snatch of words when Russell felt that they weren't too silly, and she heard them in Russell's fair Italian. She herself knew the English and filled it in soundlessly.

They call me venal
They call me corrupt
But I don't sell myself for money to pretty women
No. . . . No!

At this point, she knew, came a cynical laugh, but Charles
Russell had not attempted it. The ommission was unimportant since the ghosts of a thousand basses supplied its echo.

If I must break my sacred oath
I want other reward for it, other reward

And perfectly rightly at that, she thought. Scarpia had
been grossly misjudged. So far from being a shocking villain
he'd been a respectable civil servant doing his job, and if
that job had been suppressing liberty, well, it had been the
Romans' liberty. They didn't know what that was and they
never would. As for picking a woman up on the way, that
bitch of a Tosca had asked for it. Since he'd wanted her, of
course he'd take her, though God knew why, the woman
was dumb, the girl of some well-born but tiresome painter.
But the best of Spanish luck to him just the same.

È vin di Spagna
Un sorso per rincorarvi

So she sticks a dirty great knife in his chest and the audience approves of it. Fools. That wasn't the message to Julia
Hartley.

'The first turning on the left,' she said.

'I know.'

They coasted quietly past the lodge up the curving drive,
the headlights off. It was beautifully kept as was everything
else, the house freshly painted, the policies perfect. The
rhododendrons were trimmed to an inch of their lives, in
the garden behind not a weed out of place. Charles Russell
smiled sourly. He knew that all this was on Agnes's money
and the late Agnes Omerod, unfaithful but charming, would
have thought it a very poor way to spend wealth. Her own

tastes had been more informal as it was certain that her daughter's were.

They stopped at the portico : the house was in darkness. Russell said softly :

'Servants still sleeping out, I see.'

'Father won't be served by foreigners and the others are hard to persuade to sleep in.'

'It's asking for trouble.'

'I know it is, and the police don't like it.'

'I suppose they won't have a man around?'

'They haven't the people—they told us so. A man calls to check just once a week, but since you could set your clock by his visits I don't suppose they're the slightest use. It's ritual action—positively Indian. Tonight's not his night in any case.'

'Good.'

She unlocked the front door but they left the lights off. Russell had brought a hooded torch which he swung cautiously round the hall and waited.

'You know where the safe is?' Julia asked him.

'I do indeed.' He smiled as he spoke for he hadn't forgotten. Another incident at Omerod's safe had tickled Charles Russell's sense of drama.

They went into the study together and Julia took the torch from Russell. When the beam was on the dial she said :

'One-seven. Three-five. Four-nine.'

He set the dial and pulled on the handle. The door of the safe stayed firmly shut.

He looked at her uncertainly. 'I suppose you couldn't have changed the combo? After that other affair, I mean.'

'But of course I did—I changed it next morning. I did it myself and that's the new one.'

'Did you write it down?'

'In my notebook. I haven't brought it.'

'Awkward.'

She said apologetically : 'We're stuck? I've managed to make a stupid nonsense?'

'I'm afraid I'm not a peterman and we didn't think of bringing one.' He spoke without a hint of annoyance and her opinion of him, already high, rose strongly that he hadn't snapped.

'I'm sorry,' she said, 'I really am. I've let you down disgracefully.'

'Just wait while I think.' He was still unmoved but he swung on her suddenly. 'What's my telephone number, please? And quick.'

'I don't remember.'

'I think you do. Try.'

'Welbeck,' she said. 'Three-two-eight-six.'

'Excellent. Except that it isn't. It's Welbeck Three-two-six-eight.'

'If you're trying to prove I've a very poor memory—'

'I'm trying to prove no such foolishness. In a six-figure number there are a hundred and twenty permutations, assuming that you use all the numbers and none of those numbers more than once. We haven't time for that nor I the patience. But if you've simply *transposed* a pair, as you did about my telephone—'

'We've got a hope?'

'It's just worth a try. I'll reverse the first pair and leave the rest.'

He reset the dial and the safe stayed shut.

'I'm sorry, Charles—'

'Be quiet.' He had started to talk to himself in a monotone. 'One-seven. *Five-three.* Four-nine.'

A pull again. Nothing.

'One-seven. Three-five. *Nine-four.*'

The door of the safe swung smoothly open. Inside were the diaries, bound in morocco. In the beam of the torch the leather glowed.

'Charles, you're a genius.'

'Charles, he's a bridge-player. That means he knows the odds. He plays them.'

She scooped up the diaries and Charles Russell shut the safe again. He was thinking that this time he needn't kick it.

Back in the car he started his drill. . . . Safety-belt and the passenger's too. Then the key half right and check again. Petrol—plenty. Water temperature normal. Oil pressure would show when the engine started. . . .

85

A man put a gun through the open window.

The man from Fifty-five had lost his nerve. In any other profession this would have been understandable since he'd suffered a wholly horrible evening. To begin with he was a desk-man now, his days as an operator long behind him, but it was the height of the holiday season and his masters had been short-handed as usual. So they'd told him it would be perfectly simple. The man Bull called It had briefed him himself. . . . A piece of cake, old boy, a piece of cake. All you have to do is to watch the house. You've done worse than that before, ha-ha, and the Foreign Office is probably flapping. They usually do, God rot their guts, so it's a hundred to eight that nothing happens. But if it does, use the minimum force, no more, just *discourage* the bloke from breaking in. It'll probably be some amateur and you'll know perfectly how to deal with him. That's our brief and I mean to stick to it. Okay?

The man from Fifty-five said Okay, but it hadn't turned out like that at all. To start with it hadn't been amateur—he'd realized that from the other man's movements. He'd walked quietly, well-gloved, carrying what looked like a doctor's grip, moving ominously professionally. There'd been two of them when they'd walked out together, but the second had left the first at the window, retreating back into Fifty-five's shrubbery. He frowned in some doubt. The pair had been within yards of him and he simply hadn't heard or seen them. Had they noticed *him*? He suspected they had. Which would mean that they didn't give a damn, they were going ahead in spite of him. In any case they were two to one.

His confidence ebbed but not his courage. Indeed he felt affronted and he wasn't a man to suffer insult. . . . Two to one was too many so he'd have to reduce it. That shouldn't be impossible. He still had excellent night-sight and he hoped he could still move silently. He must take the second man first and then he'd see. That would mean leaving the other to work, but he hadn't looked the type to go smashing a window. He'd do the job as his trade dictated and that would take perhaps four minutes.

Fifty-five began stalking the Viscount Lissdale. For a desk-man he did it surprisingly well, getting within two paces without a sound. His guess that the others had seen him was wrong and Lord Lissdale was entirely off guard. He swung as some instinct warned him too late, his face as white as a winding sheet in the quarter light of a fading moon. Fifty-five had never seen him before and in any case he'd made up his mind.

He clubbed the Viscount Lissdale neatly, catching him as he fell to prevent a noise.

He put Lissdale down and stood breathing deeply. His confidence was returning now. So far so good. He crept, silently still, to the edge of the shrubbery. The first man had the window open, one leg across the sill, the other moving.

Fifty-five began to run—he had to. Inside the house he'd lose all advantage. He sprinted across the lawn and the other heard him. He put his first leg back and he turned with a gun.

Fifty-five came on fast for he wasn't a coward, and the man watched him behind the levelled gun, not uttering but holding it steady. When that didn't work he smiled and shrugged. He put the gun back in his pocket quickly. Then he stood ready, relaxed, his hands hanging.

From the moment he touched him Fifty-five knew the worst. This man was his equal and maybe his better. He tried to break Fifty-five's arm and nearly made it, then he tried for a quick rupture and almost got that. Fifty-five was in a fight and knew it, but his skills were coming back to him and he was still very hard for a man of his age. What was worrying him was how far he need go : this man was much too good just to go on blocking. Hell.

Fifty-five saw the next move just in time and he put in the counter instinctively. The man made a sound, half gasp half sob, then he fell to the ground, not trying to breakfall.

Fifty-five took his pistol, not ashamed he was trembling.

From the front of the house came a sound he recognized, a car door shutting cleanly and firmly. No one was trying to hide that noise and the no one was alas unknown. So there hadn't been only two, there were more. . . .

Fifty-five ran round to the front of the house. The courtesy light in the car was on and Fifty-five could see it all. A man was strapping a woman in and the woman was holding what looked like books. He was shaken and hadn't time to think but he did have a gun and a second's advantage.

He put the gun through the open window and waited, a thing he'd been taught he must never do.

Russell looked at the gun and the man behind it. He seemed to be considering and Julia Hartley hadn't spoken. Finally he asked blandly:

'Are you English?'

The voice had been mild but the authority came through with it. Fifty-five answered by nodding silently.

'I ask because your weapon isn't. If it interests you you've still got the safety on.'

The man behind the gun looked down.

'That was very poor drill but it's not important. I saw you at a joint conference once so at least I know where you come from.'

'Who are you, please?'

'My name's Charles Russell.'

Fifty-five looked at him. 'Please take your cap off.'

Charles Russell did so and Fifty-five froze. 'Good evening, sir,' he said at last.

'Good morning to you, or not so good. The lady with me is Mrs Hartley and also Sir Fenton Omerod's daughter. That makes a difference.'

'I'm afraid I don't follow.'

'No? Then I'll save us too much talk by guessing. Since I know where you come from I can guess what you were after. I don't ask why you were sent nor at whose request, but as you'll have noticed you're a little too late. What we have here are Fenton Omerod's diaries.'

'But it isn't like that at all, I'm afraid.'

'Indeed?'

The man from Fifty-five had made his decision: since this was Charles Russell he'd better be truthful. Moreover he badly needed help; he'd just killed a man and he hadn't meant to. 'I wasn't sent here to get those diaries but to stop

88

other people doing just that. I didn't hear you arrive, I was watching the terrace. You did it all very quietly, too.'

'Then you saved us all embarrassment.'

'Not to all of us—not to myself. There was another pair trying to break in at the back. I stopped them.'

'But that was your job.'

'The trouble is I had to kill one.'

Charles Russell said with extreme severity: 'You shot him?' He was utterly outraged at the gaffe. He had a low opinion of Fifty-five but he hadn't yet heard they'd decayed into this.

'No, this is his gun—I took it afterwards. The trouble was he knew his stuff, he knew how to maim and I had to prevent him. It was him or me so I did what I must.'

'I see. . . . And the other one of the pair you mentioned?'

'I clubbed him first.'

Charles Russell reflected, then made up his mind. He was supposed to be in well-earned retirement. 'I shall leave this to you since you seem to have started it.'

Julia hadn't spoken through this but now she began to get out of the car. 'If there's really a body in father's garden we ought at least to see if he's dead.'

'He'll be dead all right if our good friend says so.' Russell looked at her hard, approving her calm. He hadn't expected otherwise but it was better to be sure she'd take it. Even the steadiest women sometimes didn't. 'Have you ever seen a dead man before?'

She shook her head.

'There won't be blood or anything nasty, but they do look surprisingly *small*—remember that.'

They went round to the back of the house with Russell's torch. A man was lying limp on the terrace, his face against the expensive flagstones. Russell knelt down and took his shoulders, turning him round with apparent ease. The head moved last and not all the way.

'I'm glad you were telling the truth—no shooting.'

'I had to do that—he nearly got me.'

Charles Russell let this go by without comment. First he believed it and secondly the man was dead. 'Do you know who he is?' he asked at last.

'I've never seen him before but look at his face. He's one of those Slavs, I'm sure of that.'

Russell, who knew the jargon, smiled. 'One of those Slavs' was pure Fifty-five. His Excellency and Josef Satra had once used another and bitterer word.

There was a silence till Fifty-five at length broke it. 'I'd be grateful for your advice if you'll give it.'

'I really don't think you need it much. How hard did you hit the other one?'

'He'll come round in a bit.'

'Then you're something more than merely lucky. They always use more than one man, as you've found, so when the second comes round he'll take this one away. There's an understanding about each other's misfortunes.' Fifty-five was looking incredulous and Russell began to explain it quickly. 'It's done out of Hull, the port of Hull. There's a great deal of fishing done out of Hull, and other things often much more profitable.' He was looking at Fifty-five with interest, for to Russell he seemed surprisingly ignorant. That was just like Fifty-five of course, the compartmentalized over-secretive mind.

'You mean I really do nothing, sir?'

'I do. Go straight back to your base and report what's happened. You can mention my name since you certainly ought to. You should also say that I've got the diaries. Your own people may not care about those, but whoever asked for their help most certainly will.'

'And that's all I need do?'

'Not quite, I'm afraid.' Charles Russell had risen but looked down at the body. 'Do you think this one knew you?'

'I didn't know him.'

'In any case he's extremely dead. But the other one, the one you clubbed. Do you think he managed to see your face?'

Fifty-five waved an arm at the silent shrubbery. 'I took him in there and that's where he's lying. It was pretty dark and I doubt if he saw much.'

'You should very sincerely pray he didn't. I told you there was an understanding, an understanding for each side's accidents. But they're never forgotten and never forgiven. Remember that well if you want to live.'

'I will, sir.'

'Good luck.'

They returned to Russell's car without him and Russell drove back to London fast. He wasn't humming now but thinking. There was a question which she must ask him though, and she asked it as they reached her friend's flat.

'There's a man dead already because of those diaries—'

'I'll keep them for the moment—yes. I've a safe of a sort in my flat for tonight, and I'll take them down to the bank in the morning.'

'For God's sake be careful,' she said.

'I will.'

CHAPTER TEN

Russell was calling on Harry Tuke as he'd already told Julia Hartley he meant to, his motive now more urgent for what had happened in the small hours. Tuke was no longer Russell's Minister but the two were very good friends indeed. They were men from entirely different worlds but each understood the other perfectly. Tuke was a politician, a pro; he had fought his way up through his party's jungle, and now he was one of the handful who counted. The hungry Twenties had scarred him deeply but he had a vast contempt for theory still, an ever-ready and blistering word for what he classed together as clever boys. He was a very good Minister, still an entirely human being; he administered since that was part of the job, but he worshipped at no collectivist shrine and loaded clichés like social justice made him snort. His civil servants adored him.

He thought of Charles Russell with real affection, and privately used a private label. This emphatically wasn't gentleman. Gentlemen were terrible bores and when it came to the pinches you couldn't trust them, but Charles Russell was something else and something more. A patrician perhaps, the word wasn't so silly, but whatever you called him the fact remained. You could talk to Charles Russell, he'd understand you. He could sometimes be very tough indeed, but instinctively he thought first of people, dimwitted and perfectly ordinary people, not units in some planner's dream, not to be pushed around just to tidy up. To the conscientious pragmatist, and Harry Tuke sincerely was one, Charles Russell was more than friend, he was natural ally.

Harry Tuke had listened carefully, then he picked up a pencil and licked the point. He knew that the habit was unbecoming but he'd never even tried to break it. The pencil wrote better so what the hell. He wrote clearly and simply but hardly with elegance. He didn't give a fig for elegance. When the words he wrote were going outside he had civil servants to polish them for him, and when he was writing to clear his mind, to hand across a desk to Russell, it really didn't matter a damn if the fact came out plain that he wasn't much educated.

1. *Bloody man Omerod knows something he shouldn't. Means to put it in a book and publish. Probable motives fame and malice. Never got to the top and didn't deserve to.*
2. *If this book comes out it'll bust a country. It'll also put this one up the creek. This Omerod was our man and we can't escape it.*

He handed this deathless prose to Russell. 'Is that correct so far?'

'Alas, correct.'

Tuke took back the paper, re-licking the pencil.

3. *It all seems to depend on these flaming diaries. The country they're going to damage is scared, so it's had a shot at scaring Omerod. Whether that will have worked we don't yet know. But now there's also a country which WANTS publication, so if Omerod does chicken it wants the diaries. It's already had a shot at them. Happily you got there first.*
4. *But so did a man from Fifty-five and that's the worst news I've had for weeks. Fifty-five is the bottom and has been for years.*

Tuke handed this to Russell again, but he didn't write more since he didn't know it. When it came to the questions he'd rather speak. He began to put his queries clearly:

'Why do you think that man was there?'

'I'd guess not on Fifty-five's own initiative. I agree they're the bottom, but that means they don't hear things, or not till much too late to act. And I believed their man in what he said, that he wasn't after the diaries himself, only there to prevent a theft by those others.'

'Which he certainly did.'

'Not to worry about a foreign body. There's an understanding—I told you.'

'I very much hope you're right, I do indeed.'

'I'll give you twenty to one in five pound notes.'

'Not taken, or not from you, Charles.' The Minister rubbed an ample chin. 'Where were we? Ah yes. So if the initiative wasn't Fifty-five's own, who put that wretched mob in gear?'

'I was hoping you could tell me that.'

'I can't except that it wasn't me.'

'I didn't really suppose it was.'

'Then guess, damn your eyes.'

'I'd guess it was Bull.'

'The new man at the Foreign Office? Crazy.'

'I don't see why it's crazy at all. Bull's trying to pull the place together and Fenton Omerod was one of his people. Bull had probably heard of the book from the first, and later, I'd guess, he was told of the diaries. And Bull's no sort of fool whatever. He wouldn't want Omerod to publish his book but he'd be seriously frightened when he heard about the diaries. The one thing he doesn't want is another scandal and if that story broke from a *foreign* source, one of his diplomat's diaries to back it—'

'Christ.'

Harry Tuke drank a cup of extremely strong tea. His drinks were beer and tea in that order. 'I suppose it could fit,' he said at last. He sounded surprised but not incredulous; he took the paper back from Russell.

Agents of small country on the spot. Beat up Omerod to scare him off.

Another and much more powerful country. Wants the opposite of the small one.

Sir Albert Bull, Knight This, Knight that. Doesn't want the book published nor dare steal the diaries, but will call in those clowns at Fifty-five to make sure that the big boys don't get them themselves.

Colonel Charles Russell who did get the diaries. Very irregular action indeed but wisely took Omerod's daughter with him.

Russell read this in turn and nodded firmly. 'I couldn't have put it better myself.'

'You flatter me but I'm glad you agree.' The Minister frowned but not at Russell. 'It's a proper load of hay,' he said. 'You know the sort of hay I mean. Any suggestions?'

'None at all.'

'Have you read those diaries?'

'They're private papers.'

'Come off it, Charles, we're very old friends.'

'I said they were private papers. Leave it.'

'Then I'll make my suggestion which goes like this. The diaries are safe enough for a while, especially when they're down at your bank. Even our friends can't get at them there.' Harry Tuke sat up suddenly. 'But Omerod could—they're still his property. Which means we must think of the book still, just like Bull. There's plenty of time for Omerod to go stubborn and he'd certainly win if he cared to sue you. The book's being done by the Maidenhair Press?' The Minister looked at Russell innocently. This had always frightened Charles Russell severely. 'You know Peregrine Vane?'

'He belongs to my club.'

'Tell me about him.'

'He's clever and wet. Very left wing.'

'There are dozens in my party, God help us.' For the first time Tuke seemed to brighten a little. 'I know the type, they're ambitious and also inverted snobs. I'd like you to talk to Peregrine Vane.'

'God save you, Harry, he's not a Mackellar. You might do business with Steven Mackellar but never with Vane.'

'I know he's not Steven Mackellar, I wish he were. I know Steve Mackellar and like him well.'

Mackellar was head of a first-class firm, solid commercial publishing which made money. He was also the Minister's sort of man : you could talk with Steve and he'd make a price. And a very good man in foursomes too, the sort which didn't miss putts under pressure. He was five feet seven and broad to match, a civilized manner concealing his toughness. He looked like a wise and tolerant frog, an unmistakably heterosexual frog.

The Minister returned to Russell. 'So get hold of Peregrine Vane and fix him. Get him to give up the book and I'll pay. You know from where so I needn't tell you.'

'Then you'd better send a pro, not me.'

'I don't have a pro who belongs to your club.' Tuke blew his nose noisily. It was another habit he knew was vulgar and again he didn't intend to change it. 'How much do you think the damned thing's worth ?'

'In money ? It's hard to say. If it's anything like we think it is it might be a best-seller and more. Then American rights and all the rest—'

'You don't think money's the right approach ?'

'I think it's a very bad one indeed.'

Harry Tuke said reflectively : 'That sort of man has an itch to govern, so he'll probably want to get into the House. That wouldn't put him near power nor anything like it, but it's surprising what the bright boys don't know.' He drank some more tea before deciding. 'I could probably work him a nomination, a constituency in darkest Norfolk. It isn't a safe seat of course, but even Peregrine Vane won't expect that first time.'

'I still think you'd better send a pro.'

'To hell with the pros, he wouldn't trust them. Whereas Colonel Charles Russell, a fellow member—'

'What a ruthless old bastard you were and are. I'm officially fully retired and gaga.'

'Ruthless I am but not a bastard. My mother kept her lines in the bottom draw.' Harry Tuke snapped his fingers, he'd had an idea. 'I said he'd be a snob,' he said.

'What of it? They mostly are. Inside-out no doubt, but it comes to the same. Kick the Establishment's arse but wish it was theirs. There are dozens of books on that if you care to read them.'

'You can keep the books, we'll use the facts.' Harry Tuke looked at Russell, smiling blandly. 'Go down to your club, please, and contact Vane.'

'And what am I to say to him?'

'Easy. Tell him to kill the book and we'll love him. Offer him a knighthood, see?'

Satra heard the news first from a friend, another soldier. He was senior to Josef Satra, almost a man of the ambassador's age and ambience, but Satra had always admired him professionally and once he had managed to save his career. What was now this senior officer had been in very serious private trouble, not politically but quite as bad. Julia Hartley had once decided that since you mustn't call them bourgeois you could only call them Victorian, and this had been the sort of trouble which would have broken any official's career. Partly by threats and partly by money Satra had managed to shut the boy's mouth, and the senior man had never forgotten. He was making a tour now, inspecting Attachés, and had taken Satra out to dinner. There he'd repaid his debt by telling him : Satra had been in the West too long so Satra had a black mark against him. He was something more than suspect too, there was even a growing file in the He'd-Know-Where. The senior man had looked away. He'd told Satra this because he must; he told him and he destroyed his world.

Josef Satra's first feeling had simply been anger. The charge was unfair, the idea an insult. Perhaps he had been away too long, but he was anxious himself for a cleaner air and he didn't believe he was tainted—never. Of course he didn't see recent events exactly as the Ambassador did, but His Excellency was twenty years older, really a man from another age. Satra didn't wish to see that back but other men wanted the dread thing badly, and these others, he was certain now, included the grim old man himself. Let them want since they wouldn't obtain their wish; they wouldn't, that is, unless strangers imposed it, they wouldn't if Satra's own generation could keep its head and play its cards sensibly. This had nothing to do with the West or softness; it was another form of patriotism and not one to be ashamed of.

But they'd put a black mark on his name and that was final. Satra was too experienced, too wise in his own party's ways, to suppose that he could ever erase it. He wouldn't be given the chance to erase it, he wouldn't even have known it was there if his friend hadn't paid his debt in the telling.

So at first he had simply been angry and bitter, but as the waves of reality washed his feet he knew that they came from a very cold sea. . . . He'd be put on some charge and framed for treason? That was possible but unlikely since their instinct had always been to hide. So perhaps they'd quietly put him away; the thing had been done and in Satra's own lifetime. But he shook his head, though with less than certainty. Matters hadn't gone back to that just yet and with luck one could hope that they never would, but a man whose career was the army was finished. No more work in a line which fulfilled his talents, but back to a regiment he'd never command. Just another passed-over Major, a bum. He wouldn't take it.

He'd have to, though, or do something shameful, and he wouldn't even consider that.

He found that he was doing so, as a matter of theory, naturally. He'd always known about defection for he'd heard of it twice and seen it once, but it was something as remote from him as the stars in their changeless frigid courses, a possibility which didn't touch him. . . . Defection —a word, a dirty one. Only wicked men harboured the thought of it, only traitors could face the actual deed. And he wasn't a traitor, by God he wasn't.

But if they decided to think the opposite, if they treated him like the scum he wasn't? Where did a man's loyalties lie when what was returned was crude injustice? That was thinking like the West perhaps, but for once he wasn't ashamed for the West. This was simply a wrong, raw and intolerable.

And Julia Hartley—he wanted her badly. He'd thought that he'd had a very fair chance, he could see that he attracted her powerfully, and as for her husband he couldn't take Kendal seriously. He'd made inquiries about Kendal Hartley and the picture had raised that rarity, a smile. He was the typical Western intellectual, stuffed to the eyes with something called humanism, liberal and benevolent, poor. Not in money, he earned enough of that, but poor in all that made a man; he was poor in spirit. Satra had little to fear from Kendal and it wasn't gross male conceit to think so.

Little but it was everything, for Kendal Hartley was English too. She'd never come to Satra's country, Julia had made that very clear. He had put out his bait and she'd firmly declined it. Nor could he blame her for that—he didn't. She was conditioned by now and he couldn't change her. If he wanted her he must pay her price.

But that would be horrible, total apostasy, and he shrank from it both in thought and feeling. His country was far from perfect still, but he'd known it in childhood and hated the system. They'd had a president and a parliament, all the trappings of this democracy, and in the towns there'd been unemployment and in the countryside women pulled ploughs like oxen. The price they'd paid to change most of that had very nearly broken them, but paid they had and somehow survived, the weak somehow stronger, the brave still braver. For a man to turn his back on that he needed to be contemptible. He wouldn't do that because of injustice, he didn't dare do it for Julia Hartley.

... Just the same, as a matter of purest theory. ...

He made himself drunk and went to bed.

CHAPTER ELEVEN

The Ambassador had made up his mind though it had cost him some very hard thinking to do so. He had been to see Albert Bull again and this time he'd put the pressure on. If

Omerod's book came out it would break a country, but also it would damage Bull's. There wasn't an escape from that and Sir Albert Bull must realize it. Omerod had been a senior man, what was laughingly called Her Majesty's Ambassador: one simply couldn't deny the fact he was British and held an official position, so if His Excellency's country suffered, and there really wasn't much doubt it would, Sir Albert Bull would be back to the wall. Then surely here was a common interest, an occasion for Bull to use, well, his influence? He would be much too experienced to hide that such a thing existed, and His Excellency had called with a single purpose, to suggest that they travel a single road. Suggest, of course—there was nothing more. But the suggestion must come in the strongest terms, both sides had too much at stake to risk imprecision.

Bull had listened with patience and something more; he was a hard and skilful negotiator and knew perfectly how to convey without commitment. . . . He wasn't averse from the course suggested but he hadn't as yet decided the means. But the Ambassador had made his point and Bull had been impressed by it. He'd give it due thought as it clearly deserved.

His Excellency went home and thought. His case was a good one but Bull hadn't said snap. Why hadn't he agreed at once? To His Excellency the Ambassador it simply wasn't credible that a Permanent Under-Secretary couldn't quash a mere book if he really wished to; a hardliner could never conceive the thought, which was alien to his political training and offensive to his private ethos. Bull was a senior State official, one who had motive, different but potent. But he hadn't agreed at once—he'd said he'd think. Why had he said he'd think? *What did he want?*

To His Excellency it was obvious, no other hypothesis fitted the facts: Albert Bull wanted more than their common interest. He'd conceded by silence that Omerod's book could embarrass him but he hadn't conceded he couldn't ride it; he wanted more for his money and that was good diplomacy. The Ambassador wasn't resentful of it: on the contrary his opinion of Albert Bull rose.

Very well, one must pay his price, but what was it? His

99

Excellency knew nothing his country could give which Bull would want. There was no trouble between them officially, not even an English tourist in jail. So if it wasn't some quick specific payment it had to be something always acceptable. Very possibly Bull had had nothing in mind, he'd been sitting back quietly awaiting offers. And that was good diplomacy too.

When it came to the Ambassador it came with an utter and final conviction, the Tablet from the Mountain, the Law. He knew now what to offer to tip the scales. He'd offer them what they'd always accept, he'd offer them a defector. Beautiful.

Once he'd taken the major decision by instinct his mind took it over with practised ease. This was country he knew perfectly. The defections which mattered you couldn't control, but this wouldn't be the first time that some useless creature had gone with trumpets, or rather had been allowed to go. You got rid of something you didn't want and when the West woke up it found it had nothing, nothing but the publicity, though that was what it seemed to value. . . . See, yet another has chosen our way! What fools they were, what political babies.

He wrote another long dispatch home. They were going to have to pay a price but he thought he knew one acceptable. He was much too wise to mention defection. That would put them in a flap at once and almost certainly they'd veto it. Much better present the *fait accompli*, and when they found whom he'd sold they wouldn't kick. What, after all, were Ambassadors for if not to deal with local difficulties? And if by chance they saw it differently, if they called him back and broke him publicly? Then he'd die in his own country at least. He was wholly convinced he'd decided rightly, and if this was his last service then he'd answer to his conscience alone.

He smiled at a less lofty thought. There was nothing like a public defection to strengthen the hardliners' hands. He himself was one of them and this was the way he'd been taught to think.

Besides, it fitted logically and he'd been trained to respect cold logic's beauty. He was killing two birds with a single stone and that was what he believed was elegance. Not that he wasn't mildly sorry that it would have to be Josef Satra who went, but the man had gone soft, he was useless really, and if you might once allow yourself to look at a personal matter personally, he'd already been twice reported on so he hadn't a future in any case. It was better to let him go where his weakness pointed. He knew nothing that mattered, was wholly expendable. No tears for Josef Satra then, only steady contempt for those who bought him. His Excellency could even hope; he sincerely hoped the boy would be happy.

He sent for Joseph Satra again.

He had made up his mind what he wanted to say, and since he was cunning, how to say it. He began rather formally, the senior both in diplomacy and their Party. He was sorry to be obliged to say it but he'd had to report on Satra adversely. That memorandum had been past forgiving but had also been the climax of another and more disturbing disease. What disease? A perfectly legitimate question and Major Josef Satra was owed an answer. So he'd been in the West too long for his good, he was picking up strange ideas, worse habits. The word might seem a trifle severe but Josef Satra had been infected. It was time he went home lest the sickness prove fatal.

The Ambassador watched him accept this in silence. Satra didn't seem greatly surprised and he didn't protest. That was wholly unexpected for the words were an insult to any good communist and a kick in the teeth to a serving soldier. For a moment the old man lost his stride, for a thought had occurred which he didn't relish. Satra was taking this coolly because he knew : somebody had forewarned the man. The Ambassador had wondered once—were they really still secure at home, were his coded dispatches as safe as they should be? If that was the answer he was out on a limb, and if it had been a private leak the position could be even worse. For then someone had put a personal feeling ahead of what was his Party duty and that meant the whole machine was collapsing. His Excellency's world had begun to crumble.

So for a moment he lost his stride but recovered it, moving smoothly into his second lap. This was a naked appeal to patriotism and the Ambassador did it perfectly because the words which it suited him well to use were emotions which he genuinely felt. But first came a gentle softening up. . . . Of course it would be embarrassing to go home under this sort of cloud; a man might be apprehensive and worse. At the lowest there'd be a long reconditioning and there was no guarantee of re-acceptance. There'd always remain that black mark standing, a terrible query against his name. Yes, a man might think twice about going home, especially if he could still do a service. An enormous service, one to his motherland. Never mind about the Party for once, think of the country and think like a man.

Satra had so far listened in silence but now he asked the question he must. 'What do you want me to do?' he said.

'I want you to defect to the West.'

'But that would be a shameful thing.'

The Ambassador had been listening carefully, less to the words, which he'd fully expected, than to Satra's tone, the way he said them. He had spoken almost impersonally, stating the fact that this would be shameful; he hadn't said it would shame Josef Satra, he hadn't let loose a flood of protest, above all he hadn't simply stalked out. His Excellency had the feel of it now, it was swinging his way, the man was thinking.

'You wish to know why I ask this service?'

'If Your Excellency elects to tell me.'

'You've every reason to know the motive for what on its face may look like treason.' The Ambassador thought again, choosing his words. 'You know about this book of Omerod's and you know what it could do to us. Bull could stop it if he wanted to—they're not as weak and as rotten as that. In fact I'm perfectly sure he's tempted.'

'Of course he could stop it,' Satra said. Like the Ambassador he hadn't a doubt. It was inconceivable a state existed where one of a dozen top officials couldn't manage a trifle like stopping a book. 'Why doesn't he, then?'

'He wants his price.'

'A defector?' Satra nodded at once for he'd understood. His own world prized defectors highly and it went to enormous pains to obtain them. Naturally Bull would think the same.

But His Excellency was talking again. 'It isn't as though you had real information—I wouldn't suggest such a course if you had. You know little about our organization and nothing about the networks at all. But you're a Military Attaché and as such you're an acceptable prize.'

'You don't mean prize, you mean a burnt offering.'

'An offering on our country's altar.' The voice changed quickly, suddenly sharp. 'About the last which it lies in your power to make.'

'I'd prefer that you didn't threaten me.'

'I'm not threatening you but stating a fact. I put it before as mildly as possible but you'll know very well what could also happen. The Major Josef Satra is finished.'

'Except for this one last service?'

'Yes.'

'Of course I can't do it.'

'At least you'll think?'

'As you put it you make it my duty to think.'

His Excellency relaxed, he was winning now; he was out in the final lap and leading and he still had his last high ace in hand. His voice changed again to friendliness, an older man helping a younger's dilemma. 'In England there'd be a compensation.'

'If you think I'd defect for a woman you think quite wrong.'

'I think nothing so stupid, why should I so think? If you'd been made like that you'd have gone by now, but there's something else you told me once. You told me that you had acted in fear, in sending that unforgivable memo. You said you were fearful for Julia Hartley.'

'I was and I am.'

'*And so am I.*'

Josef Satra was standing, silent but menacing.

'Sit down please, and listen.'

'You mean you've had orders which put her in danger?' He got the words out but only just.

The Ambassador hated lying and didn't. 'You can't expect me to tell you that, but I'm telling you your own thinking was sound. What you deduced was entirely orthodox. If you fail with a man then you go for the woman.'

'Oh God,' Satra said.

'Who I doubt will assist her. What she needs is protection, what she needs is a man. A man of her own at constant call.'

There was a long charged silence which Satra broke. 'I didn't even know you'd met her.'

'I haven't, or not recently.' His Excellency looked at his broken nails. 'Let me tell you a little story,' he said. 'You know I was in this country before, as a very young man and very poor. I had a rich woman friend whom I've never forgotten. She wasn't a virtuous woman—no. She was married and shamelessly horned her husband. But she was honest and tender, a giver too. You remember that sort as old age comes down. She was a giver all right and she gave me a daughter.'

'What are you trying to say to me now?'

'That I'm Julia Hartley's father and I'd like to see her safe and happy.' His Excellency stood up suddenly, no longer young but no man to fool with. 'If you ever dare to let her down I'll come back from the grave and murder you.'

Charles Russell went down to his club that evening but it wasn't Peregrine Vane whom he met. The hall porter came out of his box by the door.

'There's a gentleman waiting to see you, sir.'

'I don't remember an appointment.'

'He said he didn't have one but he was hoping to catch you on something important. He looked all right so we put him in the morning-room.'

'What was his name?'

'Lord Lissdale, sir.'

Lord Lissdale got up as Charles Russell came in. 'It's kind of you to see me,' he said.

'Not at all. Would you like a drink?'

'Very much and I'd like it now if I may. When I've said what I have to I doubt if you'd offer one.'

'Is that so?'

Charles Russell inspected Lord Lissdale with interest. He

knew all about the Viscount Lissdale as he knew all about Lord Lissdale's kind. What interested him was not the record but the look of Lord Lissdale who sat before him. Russell knew a scared man when he saw one plainly.

He had reason to be scared and more for Crophead had been severe with him. Lord Lissdale, he'd said, had quite often been useful but he'd be very unwise to presume on that. He was far from indispensable, on the contrary he was expendable, and expended was what he'd certainly be if he went on mismanaging simple affairs. Look at recent events —they made a man blush. Lord Lissdale's first task had been perfectly simple, to convey a clear message to Colonel Charles Russell, a familiar one he'd at once understand. And Lissdale had surely muddled that since Russell, so far from accepting this message, had taken a direct hand himself. With results which could only be called disastrous. A valuable life had been fruitlessly lost and Russell now held the diaries himself. Crophead wouldn't waste time in re-crimination but he held Lord Lissdale fully responsible. His instructions, then? He had no instructions. It was only the diaries which mattered now. Lord Lissdale had made this mess—clean it up. Lord Lissdale would clean it up or else.

So Charles Russell watched Lissdale drink his whisky, waiting for him to make his move. He said at last simply:

'Fenton Omerod's diaries.'

'What about Sir Fenton Omerod's diaries?'

'We know you have them.'

'How do you know?'

'I was there when you took them from Omerod's house. I saw you drive away with them.'

Charles Russell would have liked to laugh. 'You were the other man there, the one who got clubbed?'

'That clown of yours hit me pretty hard but I came round in time to see you go.'

'If I wasn't your host I could wish he'd hit harder. As it happens he wasn't mine at all but I don't suppose you'll believe me.'

'If this wasn't your club I should say I didn't. However, I'm not concerned with that farce. I'm interested in the diaries, though. You have them—we want them.'

'I realize you want them and also why. You're frightened of Omerod's changing his mind, in which case you'll want the diaries yourselves.'

'If you realize that you'll realize it's serious.'

'Yes,' Russell said, 'it's very serious.'

'For you, I meant.'

'I took your meaning.'

The faintest suspicion of self-approval and Russell was at once on guard, but it was permissible to savour quietly that an experienced guess had turned out right. They *had* been seeking to warn him off and it wasn't a message which Russell resented. He had had it several times before and had even on occasion complied, since he'd never considered it sensible to invoke the Executive's delicate power when the interests of his country were anything less than directly at stake. That wasn't what it was for at all. The big boys did steal your wicket sometimes and they played on it very rough indeed, but provided they didn't break your windows it was simply an unfraternal fuss to object to the sort of game they played.

That was often true but not in this case. Russell's country did have an interest here, responsibility for Omerod's diaries, the finger of shame inescapably pointed when his book destroyed a friendly people. But if they'd thought of that aspect they'd have promptly dismissed it : public opinion was something important so public opinion wasn't *realpolitik*. Russell tasted the arrogance quietly, the irony too. So they'd sent him a message to stay on the sidelines, in their ethos an obvious thing to do, and as matters had broken they'd assume he'd declined it. They had tried to take Fenton Omerod's diaries and the theft had been prevented by force. *Ergo* Charles Russell had warned the Executive, he'd put the machine in gear and they'd lost a life. That was beautifully logical, beautifully wrong. And it would never have occurred to them that the message was in fact unnecessary, that the last thing he'd risk would be action by the Executive, action against Sir Fenton Omerod, whom Russell might well despise and detest but was also the father of Julia Hartley. They had very good minds within given premises but outside them they were as blind as bats. All men of religion were blind as

106

bats and these had been trained in the strictest of all. Russell hadn't informed the Executive, not even hinted; he had feared what might happen to Fenton Omerod. But they wouldn't have thought of that in a hundred years. Instead they'd go forward in splendid blind logic, which meant that they'd start to threaten him.

Lord Lissdale began to do so smoothly. 'We know you haven't been down to your bank.'

'You've been shadowing me?' He was properly curious. 'I'll admit that you've done it pretty well.'

'Of course we did it well—we've the means. And means to do more than tail a man.'

'You're telling me something I know,' Russell said.

'Then why not be sensible? Give us those diaries.'

'And what do you suggest in return?'

'Nothing beyond the negative—your personal safety. You're not young any more and you're no longer in a certain chair. You don't have a man to carry a gun when guns or anything like them are needed. You haven't got what you had and you know it.'

'And so?'

'You'd be well advised to do as I ask.'

Charles Russell finished his drink deliberately. He saw that Lissdale's was finished too but he didn't propose another one. Instead he rose.

'You must forgive me now, I've another appointment.' It wasn't quite true but a social lie. He saw Lord Lissdale out politely, then went down to the washroom and washed his hands carefully. That done he took a taxi home. He now had much more urgent business than waiting about for Peregrine Vane.

Back in his flat he opened the wall-safe, taking out Fenton Omerod's diaries. He had told Harry Tuke they were private papers but in fact he'd had no compunction in reading them. Men's lives were at stake, not a private convention.

He still had two to finish and these, he suspected, the worst of all. He read them now attentively, then closed the last with a final snap. He'd made up his mind, he needn't think. The bank was not the place for these.

He walked down the stairs of the maisonette, knocking at

his housekeeper's door. Nobody answered and Russell remembered. It was the lady's night out and she'd have gone to that club of hers. There she got mildly tight and talked Gaelic. He didn't object to that once a week and indeed thought she'd decently earned it.

The door wasn't locked and he went through her quarters, out into the service courtyard. The back had been recently modernized and in a concrete shed he found what he wanted. There was even a long steel handle to open the door.

He opened it quickly and did what he must.

It was a very dull party and she'd gone to it professionally, knowing that she'd be cruelly bored but also that she'd be paid for it. Julia Hartley looked round the room and sighed. There were the usual diplomatic faces, smooth and a little defensive, tired. There was also Josef Satra and his face was neither smooth nor tired. She hadn't consciously wished to meet him again but she'd known it was inevitable, and in her woman's heart she was also curious. How did a man like that behave when he'd put down his hand and you hadn't responded? Did he take his *congé* or did he fight back? A part of her hoped that he'd leave her in peace but another part hoped that he wouldn't avoid her. Julia was a successful journalist but she was also a woman and pleased to be one.

He left her in no doubt at all, striding across the room at her, buoyant and vigorous, a man amongst half-men. In the ordinary way he'd have lifted her spirits, but though he didn't know it he'd mistimed his moment disastrously. For again she'd received a letter from Kendal and this one had upset her badly.

'I must talk to you,' he said at once.

'Not here.'

'Then where?'

'I'll ring.'

She watched him with something approaching anger, but anger against herself, not at him, this splendid male creature who moved her but didn't, who made her catch her breath but guard her mind. And she'd just had shocking news from Kendal. His contract had been terminated under some small-print clause he hadn't much studied, believing that other academics were unlikely to stab their own kind in the back. The contract had seemed a standard one, and though his lawyer hadn't liked it much he'd also said that they'd hardly change it. So Kendal had signed and now they'd sacked him, but he suspected there was much more than that; he suspected he'd never work again, or not in this country he found so alien. He'd have to use a cliché since there wasn't another word for it. He suspected that he'd been blacklisted.

His first letter had annoyed her and this one had made her furious. But the difference wasn't one of degree. The first letter had made her cross with Kendal, irritated at his silly conscience, infuriated that he couldn't just *cope*. But what this one had told her was very different : she was Kendal Hartley's wife still, a partner. How dare they behave like this to her! Would they never grow up? Barbarians.

There was a discreet disturbance across the room, a fluttering of butterfly wings. Albert Bull had come in so the feast was crowned, for no host could be sure of Albert Bull. He loathed this sort of official party and avoided them when he possibly could, and even when protocol made him accept he'd been known to telephone later and blame his Minister for his absence. Ministers were inconsiderate—a *cher collègue* would naturally understand. That was part of Bull's simple technique and it worked. He was a great man for simplicity when simplicity had a chance of success.

Julia watched him with a journalist's eye. Normally he was pleasantly friendly, not tiresomely jovial but he did like to meet people. Even from a party like this he could mostly extract some quiet amusement, but this evening he seemed relaxed, almost gay, accepting a drink at once and smiling. He had reason, he thought, to enjoy a drink since the man he called It had been back to see him and the Executive had beaten them to it. It had been crestfallen, Bull had not. If Charles Russell of all men now held the diaries they would hardly reach hands which Bull had feared, and though Omerod could still make trouble Russell had won one essential, time. Bull had time now to deal with Omerod's book, time and a weapon he meant to use. Satra nodded across the room at him.

'Do you know Albert Bull?'

'I've met him, that's all.'

'Do you think you could introduce me?'

'Shouldn't your own Ambassador do that?' She had spoken it lightly, expecting a smile, perhaps even some joke though hardly a good one. But he took it in blank solemnity. 'No, the worst man possible. In any case, he isn't here.' He returned to his suggestion, pressing her. 'If you know him at all—'

'I don't know him nearly well enough.'

'Just as you say.'

There was something about his manner which grated: they might have been married for years, he was so tolerant. She was a woman being unreasonable and a husband who was fond of her still was riding a rough patch easily. She heard herself say sharply:

'Something's wrong?'

'Not at all. Quite to the contrary. But I've got to meet Bull and to meet him soon.'

'If your own man's not here there'll be dozens of others.'

'The last people appropriate. And I'd prefer to meet him socially first.'

'Are you trying to be mysterious?' She would have confessed to being irritated.

'No, I've had news and it's excellent news. I've a future now, *we've* got a future.'

. . . Something has happened and he thinks I've a place in it. And you couldn't laugh him out of it either; laughter wasn't a weapon with Josef Satra.

'I don't know what you're talking about.' She managed to keep her voice quite normal but inwardly was aware of crisis.

It was Josef Satra's crisis not hers. He hadn't asked her for what she'd considered giving, she owed him no debt but a decent sympathy. She admired his dedication and respected his integrity. He was also supremely male and she a woman. But she knew something now which she'd long suspected. He hadn't the ghost of a sense of humour.

'I must talk to you,' he was saying again.

'Why don't you ring and we'll fix a date.'

Another man came up and he went away, but Julia watched him move round the room. He moved purposefully from group to group, apparently mildly surprising each. Finally he was led up to Bull. Bull looked astonished but hid it at once. He nodded and made a note in a diary. Something of his gaiety left him. Sir Albert Bull had smelt more trouble.

Julia went home in a doubtful temper. She hadn't really expected copy, for diplomatic cocktail parties were very poor soil for the stuff you could print. She'd gone there troubled by Kendal's new letter and Josef Satra had whetted her worry. She'd had no idea what the man had meant and now it was pointless even to wonder. She'd decided now and decided finally : he wasn't for her and he never would be. In none of the possible ways, no none.

In the flat she picked a cable up, seeing at once it was quite a long one. If Kendal was sending her that sort of message it might have been simpler to ring her up. She suppressed the thought at once for that wasn't Kendal. He was far from mean but was careful of money and he'd have worked it out to a dollar or less, which would be cheaper, to ring or cable. Besides, if he rang he might not get her.

She read the cable with mounting fury. Kendal hoped she'd received his last letter all right—there'd been developments since which affected her too. A strange little man had called one evening, and when challenged where he came from he wouldn't say. But he'd hinted though, and that was enough. There was something wrong with Kendal's visa, something irregular when first he'd applied for it. That could be very serious—oh yes, it could be serious, brother. Illegal entry was rightly frowned on, and when the visitor didn't co-operate either, what was more shot his mouth about none of his business. . . . And of course it was very unwise to make foolish friends. Kendal's friends were well known where the little man came from, and candidly they weren't highly considered. Of course if he liked to face it out, to go running to his consulate with some tale which would be flatly denied. . . . But if the little man might offer advice. . . .

Kendal Hartley hadn't waited for it. He had packed his

bags and booked a sea passage. He would in fact be in England next week. He was sorry to break their understanding.

Julia read this three times and began to laugh. It was a squalid little story but it no longer made her angry. She knew Kendal Hartley. Kendal would stick his neck out on principle and naturally they'd chopped his head off. That was over-reaction—she didn't blame them. The man could be infuriating. He infuriated Julia Hartley.

But also he could make her laugh. Through the telegraphese came Kendal's humour, ironic and dry and a trifle donnish. God damn the man, he thought this funny.

The point was she thought it funny too.

Josef Satra was not amused at all but Josef Satra seldom was. He had made up his mind or had had it made up for him, and now an appointment with Bull next morning. The word for what had happened to him was there in his bible and therefore respectable. All this was ineluctable. Freedom was the recognition of what was in fact necessity. He would therefore do what he had to do since he hadn't in practice the option not to. It was as simple as that when you thought of it clearly.

He went home and to bed, this time quite sober.

CHAPTER TWELVE

At half past midnight Russell was thinking of bed at last. He had been out to dinner with friends but had not enjoyed it, haunted by the thought of Lissdale—not by what the unhappy man had said for Charles Russell had been threatened before and by persons much more formidable than a renegade English Viscount, but by the look of him, the desperation which rode him. Russell partly discounted the threats as bombast, but he'd seen too much to ignore them completely. The affair was nicely balanced now and next morning he'd talk to Tuke again, but desperate and certainly frightened men weren't considerate of the equilibrium. They were capable of foolish deeds; Russell couldn't think what but the danger remained, and any brash and premature action now could remove the matter from competent hands, Harry Tuke's, for instance, and even his own, landing them with a public scandal, the need for open political action which Russell deplored and Tuke would detest.

There was a knock on the door and Russell sighed. So his housekeeper had got tighter than usual and, losing her key, had had to knock.

He opened the door and two men pushed past him. He'd never seen either before in his life, but one was white and the other coloured. The white one shut the door behind him and the coloured tripped Russell neatly and painfully. He then threw him into his own armchair. On Russell's favourite pie-crust table he laid out a rubber truncheon, grinning.

Russell smiled too but for different reasons. For thirty years he'd controlled the Executive and seen violence perhaps six times and gunplay twice. He'd never been an operator and would have thought it an impertinence to intrude himself on the work of experts. He had given the orders, he'd sometimes been present, but he'd thought it his duty as well as good sense to let professionals handle professional matters. And now it was creeping up on him; in gentle retirement the violence had caught him. All in a matter of days at that. First a gun in his back at Omerod's villa, then another through the Mercedes's window. And now men in his flat with a rubber truncheon. The Colonel Charles Russell, Retired, had not.

The irony tickled a part of his mind but another was listening hard and carefully. Whitey was saying gratingly:

'Where are they?'

'What?'

'Those diaries of course. We know you haven't been to the bank.'

'I've been told that already,' Charles Russell said mildly.

'We want them then, and we mean to have them.'

'May I offer you a drink while we talk?' The fall had shaken him but not severely and there was a bell-push on the wall by Russell's chair. He could reach it and did so.

Whitey sneered. 'That won't do you any good at all. Your housekeeper's out, we've checked on that. Anyway, an elderly woman—'

The coloured said : 'Cut the cackle, man.'

'All right, so I will. Give us those diaries and give them quick.'

'I'm afraid I don't have them now, though I did.'

'You're a liar.'

'I'll open my safe if you wish—you can look. And you can search the flat as well if you like.' It could do no harm and time was important.

'Open your safe, then.'

Charles Russell opened it.

'And now we'll look round the flat as you say.' Whitey nodded at the coloured man. 'I'll do the search and you watch this one. No tricks, mind.'

'Right.'

Whitey came back in perhaps six minutes. 'Nothing,' he said, 'but I still think he's lying.' He nodded again at the coloured man and the coloured man picked the truncheon up.

'You're old, you know, you won't take much.'

'I expect you're perfectly right about that.'

'Then why take any? Why don't you just tell us?'

'I've told you as much as I mean to or can.'

The coloured man raised the rubber truncheon.

In the Security Executive the night duty officer was checking his chores. They were varied and would have astonished a stranger, and one of them was called The Lines. The Prime Minister didn't have one since there were other arrangements at Number Ten; the Foreign Secretary did. There were plenty of people with private grudges against the painfully high-minded man who held this ancient office so gracelessly. The other owners were a commentary on times which were strange and becoming stranger : the editor of a right-wing newspaper, a judge who'd handed down sentences which had made even his learned brethren blink, the biggest of all the London bookmakers (who paid heavily and happily for protection he couldn't have bought elsewhere), a princess whose public reputation was perhaps a little unkind but not very. There were seventeen of these Lines in all and their owners could press a bell if they wished. Within five to ten minutes, depending on where the caller lived, a polite young man would appear from the Executive —much less fuss than dialling 999, as discreet as any police-man and harder. The privilege wasn't granted at the whim of some self-important tycoon; it was authorized by Harry Tuke and Tuke authorized it personally.

The duty officer checked his book. In the past six months there'd been only three calls but each of them had saved a crime, in one case a crime which Tuke would have wel-comed. But they'd also saved an awkward scandal and to Harry Tuke that was more than a crime.

The officer had a moment to spare and he flipped through the pages idly. Of the seventeen Lines only six had been used and Charles Russell's was one of the other eleven. The duty officer nodded reflectively, remembering there'd been a fuss about Russell's Line. He'd protested he didn't want the thing, and anyway if the occasion arose he'd be embar-rassed to call for help in retirement. But the alarm had been installed in the end since Tuke had curtly ordered it.

The duty dog timed and initialled the book and was putting it down when the bell began to scream at him. He looked at the board where a red light was flashing. Sixteen —that was Colonel Russell's line.

He took the key from its hook by the winking light, pressing a button himself to alert his driver. Then he went to his desk and for a second he hesitated. The Executive's rules about firearms were strict: you simply didn't carry one unless specifically told to do so. Standing Orders would cover a call on a Line but they wouldn't cover a man who misused his weapon. Nothing had ever covered that. It was part of what they drilled into you when you joined. You mostly worked outside the law but you never rode above it—never. If you weren't prepared to accept that fact you'd do well to seek other employment quickly.

So he hesitated but he took his gun. He was an operator in the Security Executive which meant he'd been very care-fully chosen.

The coloured man raised the truncheon but held it. The door had opened and shut again fast and a stranger was standing against it, armed. He knew how to use his sweapon too. The coloured and Whitey looked at it. It wasn't pointing at either man but pointing where it should be, between them. The stranger by the door said sharply :

'Drop it.'

The coloured dropped it.

The newcomer looked at Russell : 'Sir?'

'I'm sorry to call you out like this.'

'An unexpected privilege. What would you like me to do, please?'

'Ring the police.'

'The police?' The duty officer was surprised and showed it.

'Why not?' Russell waved at the men who were watching the gun still. 'They're hoodlums.' He got out of his chair and stretched himself. 'I know the type by now and it's useless. They've been hired for the job and I'll guess by whom, but if you grilled them for days you'd get nothing important. They know nothing important to give us, you see. They don't belong to an organization.'

'What were they trying to do besides beat you?'

'Rob me.'

'Is that the story to the police, sir?'

'Yes. As it happens it's also entirely true.'

'But breaking into Charles Russell's flat—that's hardly, well, unremarkable.'

'I think you'll find we've sufficient credit—credit with the police, I mean. Enough to cover a routine robbery.'

CHAPTER THIRTEEN

Charles Russell was talking to Tuke next morning and had taken Julia Hartley with him. It was a sound and well-established principle that if you intended to tell a Minister that a woman now took a certain view it was wise to produce her in person and let her say so. Her father's book had once frightened Julia but now she'd moved on to hating it and had actively co-operated in what a purist might say had been stealing his diaries. So with these diaries now in responsible hands and Julia pleased to have them there the immediate heat had notably lessened. That was what Russell would say to Tuke. The affair of the night before he'd minimize, an amateur even stupid sideshow which hadn't affected the course of events. Julia's presence would speak for what mattered most.

He had found her with some difficulty, finally tracing her to her editor's office. She had in fact welcomed the interruption since her editor was embarrassing her. All his journalist's instincts had been smelling a story, and though he'd once told her he couldn't press her he was now coming very close to it. . . . Yes, certainly this was personal, Sir Fenton was her father no doubt, but also there might be a first-class story, and if one wasn't being absurdly pompous there was something called the public interest.

She had met him head on with a flat refusal, and with more than a refusal—she'd told the truth. She was thinking of giving her column up and of making a proper marriage at last. No, not with some foreign diplomat but with the man who happened to be her husband. He'd decided to leave the States and was coming home. He had numerous defects and what man hadn't? But she'd married him so she shared any failure. It was a mistake to juggle with too many balls especially when you'd no gifts as a juggler. . . . What was the editor saying now? He'd release her with extreme regret but she owed him the big one before she went, just the one big story to end on a bang. But Julia Hartley was tired of noises : that was the point of what she'd decided. It was time to think about settling down, about making a home and what went with it. She hadn't so far been brilliant at human relationships and it was time she made something of one at least. She had made up her mind and would give it a try, the fair run for its money it hadn't yet had. If the editor wished her well he could pray for her.

So she'd been glad when Charles Russell had come through urgently and now they were sitting with Harry Tuke. There was something in Russell's manner which she couldn't at first precisely place. She might not be brilliant at human relationships but had all the good journalist's observation, and though Russell was as urbane as ever her instinct was there was something else. He was insisting that the affair last night had been irrelevant to what really mattered, but under the casual Russell manner was an emotion which she couldn't pin down. She decided at last it was simply anger. Below his outward control Charles Russell was furious, and indeed he had a right to be. Julia Hartley felt a moment of pity for the man who had privately angered him.

Harry Tuke was drinking tea and thinking. He agreed with Russell's expressed opinion that the scene of the night before had changed nothing, but he couldn't resist the friendly dig.

'So there's nothing like a quiet retirement.'

Charles Russell didn't rise to it. 'You're thinking of that affair last night? It was really quite beside the point.'

'I doubt if I'd have found it so.'

'A cavalry skirmish, bush cavalry at that. I doubt if the head man knew of it and I'm certain he didn't authorize. The pair who broke into my flat were criminals, not the sort our old friends would dream of using. I can guess who employed them, and if it interests you I'll guess something else. Lord Lissdale will shortly be caned severely. The men who employ him are harder than he is and they put pressure on him to act and quickly. So Lissdale acted. But if they'd known what he intended they'd have handled it very differently, even if they'd agreed to it, which personally I take leave to doubt.'

'From which you deduce?'

'Strictly I don't deduce at all but I'm prepared to risk an inference. On the whole I think the omens are good, or they are where they point to the diaries directly.'

'I hope you're right but tell us why.'

'Lord Lissdale won't know exactly what happened—the police took his hoods off and they'll hardly try to contact him—but he'll know that his scheme fell flat on its face and he'll have to report to his masters accordingly. Who aren't Lord Lissdales, who'll start to think practically. If I do have the diaries still I'm protected, but they can't be very sure that I have. True, they know I haven't been down to my bank, but they can hardly have tailed every contact and visitor. There's the postman, the milkman, my housekeeper, casuals, and any of these could have taken them off for me. As I've often said they're pros or nothing, which implies that they play with the odds, not against them. To assault a retired official is one thing, not original or even effective, but the people who stand behind Lissdale himself use violence as doctors use the knife, which means when they think there's a hope of succeeding. If those diaries aren't with me any more—'

'They're somewhere safe?'

'Extremely safe.'

Harry Tuke thought it over and finally nodded. 'You're the man with the experience and I'm inclined to hope you're right again. But what about our other friends, the ones who aren't after the diaries directly, only desperate to suppress the book?' He turned to Julia Hartley politely. 'That's your side since Sir Fenton's your father.'

'I detest that book and it scares me stiff.'

'So Russell was saying, but it does leave some ends loose. For instance, it's not your book, they're not your diaries. Do you mind if I sound like a third-rate lawyer?'

'Ask what you like, I'll try to answer.'

Tuke permitted himself a tentative cough. 'Did your father authorize taking those diaries?'

'You know already he didn't do that.'

'Do you think he still means to go on with the book?'

'I can't be sure but we don't know he doesn't.'

'Then he could sue you for their recovery. You or Russell and probably both.'

'He could, I suppose, but I don't think he will.'

Harry Tuke hesitated. 'May I ask why?'

'Because of the scandal, his own good name.'

'Which would hardly be dragged in the public gutter by an action for the return of his property.'

'But that wouldn't be the public angle.' Julia met Harry Tuke's shrewd stare. 'Earlier this morning I was talking to my editor. He's a very experienced man and he smells a scoop. He wanted me to get it for him and naturally I said I

119

wouldn't, but if father goes on with this story I'll blow another. I'll say that I stole the diaries myself, and though I can't say why I really did it I can hint at an appalling scandal, a personal scandal, hot and strong.'

'You really feel like that about it?' Harry Tuke wasn't smooth now but deadly serious.

'I won't have my father destroy a country.'

The Minister was too wise to comment; instead he nodded and turned to Russell. 'And that seems to take care of just about everything. Would you say that we're out of this wood at last?'

'Yes. . . . But for one thing.'

'You see some loophole for further trouble?' In anybody but Harry Tuke the voice would have been ironical.

'It's hard to put it in words, to make it stick. We're in a world we don't properly understand.'

'You're perfectly right, I don't understand it.' The Minister sounded disappointed. 'The professionals won't gamble against the odds, or that's what I thought you were trying to tell me, so the diaries themselves are safe enough. And if Omerod can't get them back to use them—'

'We don't understand how they think and we never shall. We almost do but never quite. You can train yourself to a certain point, then suddenly, bang, you're a babe in the wood.' Russell's voice became reflective for he was talking of something he'd lived with for long. 'You sit at a desk for thirty years and you take in the dialetic through your pores. After a time you get quite good—good for fifty-eight minutes in every hour. You learn to put a following finger on what they themselves regard as premises, bits from their holy writ which they take for granted. After that you learn to think as they do, to move with them down the logical line. That way you can foretell their actions.' His smile was more than a little wry. 'Some of the time and sometimes most of it. Then you fall down through no fault of the logic. They'll do something entirely unexpected, something that leaves you literally breathless. Not something you'd thought of and discounted as stupid, but something that doesn't make sense at all. To you, that is, since you're only aping. You're putting yourself in their shoes, you're thinking as they do. Or so you hope. But you'll never *feel* as they do—never. They'll tell you that they don't feel at all, that only the dialectic rules them, but they do feel, they feel with passion too, and when that shot goes into the breech of the gun you can only sit back and wait for it. Afterwards they'll rationalize almost anything they've chosen to do, but that doesn't help the man who's been guessing. . . . Some astonishing over-reaction to nothing, some tough old hardliner's snap decision can make nonsense of your careful reasoning.' Charles Russell smiled for the second time but now apologetically. 'That was really quite a speech,' he said.

'I'm hoping you're exaggerating, I'm hoping we're still in your fifty-eight minutes.'

'So do I,' Russell said. 'I hope so sincerely.'

The telephone rang and Tuke picked it up. His heavy face hardened; he put down the phone. 'That,' he said harshly, 'was my colleague at the Foreign Office, that hedgepriest who meddles with foreign affairs. A Major Josef Satra has called and he's been talking to Sir Albert Bull. He has asked us for asylum, for political asylum.'

Josef Satra's appointment with Albert Bull had been at 10.45 the following morning, and exactly a minute later Bull was facing a major crisis. He wasn't without experience of enormously dangerous situations. There'd been that lunatic old man in India, the head of his own Political Service, who'd decided off his own sprung bat that the Princes must be rescued from the extinction they'd so richly earned and had gone to unheard-of lengths in trying to. Raja-itis in the Political had been every bit as endemic and ugly as Arab-itis in the Foreign Office. A future Indian Prime Minister had been obliged to threaten publicly; pensions could be withheld and would be. Albert Bull had considered the warning reasonable, he'd had little respect for degenerate princelings, and he and a handful of sensible men had blocked the old gentleman's worst excesses. Just the same it had been a close-run thing.

Which this present new crisis could hardly be : on the contrary the battle was lost from the start. Another defector.

Another one! The country couldn't accept the consequences, nor would this wretched defector's real masters.

Bull's eyebrows came down in a formidable scowl. He had realized at once that the play had changed, from the embarrassment of a silly book, then the active danger of dynamite diaries, onto the perilous ground of direct confrontation. For of course the other side would kick, they'd kick like the powerful bears they were. Two within months —they wouldn't take it; they wouldn't accept the loss of face, and when major Powers started thinking of face the coolest official was mostly helpless.

The scowl changed slowly to bitter smile. It had looked pretty good last night, he'd slept well. Charles Russell, not to mince his words, had stolen those diaries and was holding them safely. That might not be a final solution but it had bought him what Bull most needed, time. Fenton Omerod and his book remained but Bull wasn't frightened of Fenton Omerod, whose daughter had accompanied Russell when the two of them went to his house and robbed him. Bull hadn't yet thought through the implication but he could see it could be significant. Would Omerod take his own daughter to court for the return of a father's stolen property? That didn't sound much like Fenton Omerod, though a stubborn man might decide to do it. But the personal aspect aside, the publicity, Bull had been thinking politically. He'd been down to Omerod's hospital once and Omerod had brushed him off, but he hadn't known of the diaries then or he'd have handled the interview much more forcefully. Better— much better. Like Omerod, Bull had been talking to lawyers, and though the formal advice had not been so different the official lawyers had seen it differently. There were pressures at Albert Bull's disposal and the tame cats had suggested more. One at least would hit Fenton Omerod hard. He was rich enough to throw his pension but the loss of his titular tag, the Sir Fenton, would bite on him very hard indeed. That mightn't in fact be on in practice but the threat of it most certainly was, and even the hint it was being considered (and Bull would take care that it leaked where it mattered) would be something to bring up Omerod short. The whispers in his club, the strange looks. . . . He was that sort of man and God be thanked.

And now the original problem was play for children. Personal prestige was always the devil but that of a nation infinitely dangerous. Particularly a great communist nation.

For of course they wouldn't accept it – they couldn't. Satra wasn't their national by race or law but he was a man from a part of their world and a tender one. They'd fight like fiends and Bull didn't blame them. And Bull himself had much to lose. Negotiations had been dragging on, not for anything world-shaking, pre-war debts, but these would go into the fire at once if a second defection soured the air. They nearly had a few months ago and Bull had been very hard-pressed to save them. That kopeck-a-liner who'd wanted to stay here. . . .

They hadn't approved of that at all.

Asylum was now a dangerous nonsense. It had been all very well in the days of power—romantic but ineffective Italians escaping from the court of Naples, Frenchmen who'd fallen foul of Louis Napoleon. So you took them in and fussed them up, shaking hands with yourself that your country was free, answering protests by crisp little Notes. Crisp because you still had the power, the money, the ships, the trade, the men. If this had become a tradition, then, it was one which the country could well afford, but the trouble with traditions was that they lingered when their background had faded. Why should we take in the disaffected when their masters seemed to want them back? Why should a country play host to defectors? Satra wasn't an agent, he'd nothing to sell. Bull knew that well. The man who sat before him now was a man who had changed his mind, an embarrassment, millions of pounds at stake since he had. Sir Albert Bull resented it.

He looked across his desk at Satra, hiding his resentment by habit, his face the good official's mask. He wasn't prepared to risk sixpence for Satra, far less an agreement on trade and debts, but he'd had an idea and he wanted to test it. Sir Albert Bull knew his grim trade backwards.

'You wish us to protect you?' he asked.

'I didn't put it quite like that.'

'I know you didn't. *I* put it like that.'

'I don't think I'm that important, you know.'

'To be frank with you, neither do I. You're an official, though, an Attaché, a symbol. And symbols *can* be important. Dangerous.'

There was a silence while Satra thought it over. It wasn't quite going the way he'd expected, but he'd have to grasp the nettle in time. 'You're refusing my request?' he said.

'No, I didn't say that.'

'Then what are you saying?'

'That I'm the head of the Foreign Service. What you ask is for the Home Office.'

'But I came to you as a diplomat first.'

'*Cher collègue* and all that ancient flannel?'

Satra only just hid a blank astonishment; he'd heard that Bull could be very tough but he hadn't expected a verbal clubbing. 'I didn't mean that.'

'Then what did you mean?'

'I know that you don't control what I ask but I know you could almost certainly help me.'

'How could I help you? By going to the Home Office?'

'I confess the thought had crossed my mind.'

'I can't undertake to do any such thing.'

There was a silence again and Albert Bull weighed it. It was going quite well, Sir Albert decided—the man wasn't broken but clearly softened. He didn't want Josef Satra broken. 'Perhaps I might make a suggestion,' he said.

'I'd be something more than grateful for it.'

'Then are you sure you know your own objective?'

'I don't think I follow. I want a new life.'

'Just so. But what life? You're a professional soldier—not even from a technical Corps. You haven't a trade of any kind. There are newspapers which would ghost your story but when that money's finished, what?'

'I'm strong still. I could work.'

Sir Albert Bull sighed. 'Look at your hands, please. Look at them well.'

'I'd be grateful if you'd be frank with me.'

'Then I think you're mistaking your country, that's all. In the United States you'd have a much higher value.'

'I'd thought of that myself. I don't like it.'

'Then I'm afraid I cannot help you further.' Sir Albert Bull rose but Satra didn't. Satra said steadily :

'So you'll try to block my application?'

'I don't think I have to answer that.'

'State your terms, then. I'll listen.'

Sir Albert Bull sat down again. 'Have you any clothes with you?'

'Clothes?'

'You are going to need some badly at first. Go home and pack two suitcases—no more. Come back within an hour. I'll wait.'

When Satra had gone Bull picked up a telephone. He was on ground he knew now and he used it skilfully. The voice on the line asked a couple of questions and Bull answered them unhesitatingly. No, there wasn't a *quid pro quo*, he asked nothing. To Bull this was an embarrassment but to the voice on the line it might well be otherwise. A Military Attaché at that. Quite a fish if you liked those stinking waters.

The voice on the line said : 'Very interesting.'

'I've got to have confirmation at once.' Bull knew his opposite number perfectly. The American rather enjoyed being rushed, it gave him a sense of power and decision.

'Very well, then. Confirmed.'

'He'll be back in an hour.'

'We'll send a car.'

. . . He's a hooked busy fish.

'And I'd prefer you to move him out at once.'

'We've a standing two seats on the evening plane.'

'Two seats?'

'One for the man to go with him.'

'Right.'

Sir Albert Bull hung up and smiled, then he walked along the corridor. He didn't completely trust his Minister, but this was something he'd have to tell him.

Harry Tuke banged back the receiver, growling. 'That,' he said harshly, 'was my colleague at the Foreign Office. A Major Josef Satra has called and he's been talking to Sir

Albert Bull. He has asked us for asylum, for political asylum.'

Julia started to speak but Russell stopped her. He'd seen it at once as Bull had seen it : Omerod's wretched book, Sir Fenton's diaries—all this was in the dustbin now. Instead there was immediate crisis. He looked long and hard at Harry Tuke. 'Will you take him?' he asked. It was almost a whisper.

'I don't want to take him. I may be forced to.'

'I understand.'

The Minister exploded crossly. 'You don't understand, you can't understand. You're an official, not a politician. I've got to take him or give a good reason why not and that reason's got to be watertight. Every prig in the House, every briefless barrister, will jump on my neck if I just say no. And God, how I want to refuse the man. You know why. The last one was touch and go as it was and a second will just about crack it wide. But the clever boys won't think of that, or if they do they'll put principle first. Principle! Thundering great leaders, snide little articles. Loaded Questions to me as scapegoat Minister. Principle! We can't afford it.'

Charles Russell didn't comment since he rather more than half agreed. Not wholly but he saw the point. It was really a little absurd at best that the relations between political Powers should be muddied by a single man's action. 'Principle,' Harry Tuke had said. It was a suspect word to all practical men.

The green telephone rang again and Tuke took it. Russell could see him relax as he listened. He replaced it and for the first time smiled.

'Another message from the Foreign Office. Bull has been rather clever, I think.'

'He's a clever man, that Albert Bull.'

'You know what he's done?'

'How should I know?'

'He's got us off the hook, God save him. He's sold Satra to another country. They specialize in that sort of thing. I gather they were delighted to have him.'

'Don't tell me but I can guess—they would be.' Charles

126

Russell considered. 'When's he handing the willing body over?'

'He's sent him home to pack his bags.'

Charles Russell was out of his chair and standing. 'Bull's done *what*?'

'I told you. The man will need clothes, what's wrong with that?'

Charles Russell didn't answer him; he swung on his heel at Julia Hartley. 'Do you know his address?'

She started to tell him; he cut her short. 'Never mind, come with me.' He was half way to the door already.

The Minister said : 'What the hell—'

'Be quiet, Harry. Choke it.'

CHAPTER FOURTEEN

The Crophead whom Lissdale knew and feared was a formidable and a frightening figure, for this was the harsh impression he sought, a manner he carefully wore and flaunted to hide what his agents might take as weakness. This weakness was a distaste for bullying, a preference for discussing quietly; he preferred to deal with his equals, to bargain, but with agents in general and Lord Lissdale in particular it would be fatal to concede equality. He had built up for himself the reputation of ruthlessness and ruthless he could emphatically be, but put him among the men he respected and his agents, whom he mostly despised, would have known him by his appearance still but certainly not by his speech and bearing. Under the mask of a total brutality was a courteous and a reasonable man.

Nevertheless he was now very angry; in his small and severely furnished office Crophead was in an awkward crisis. Two pieces of news had put him there and he couldn't decide which he liked the least. The first was perhaps just tolerable since it didn't demand immediate action, but it was also a humiliation, a grievous and shameful amateur bungle which he felt as a personal slap in the face. Moreover if the story seeped home it could earn him something more than a reprimand from the only man on earth he feared. The head of his Bureau, the Colonel-General, had the highest respect for his colleague Charles Russell, an official and formal consideration which at moments came close to a private affection. Tell him that thugs had threatened Russell, not even professional thugs at that. . . .

That halfwit Lissdale, that dilettante. Lord Lissdale had chosen to think of Crophead as the chief of the various contacts who helped him. Crophead had sensed this but didn't resent it for the realities were on Crophead's side. Lord Lissdale was useful where others were not but his private hopes were quietly laughed at, his political pretensions absurd. He was a man with a universal entrée and he'd arranged himself really first-class cover, but his belief he was something more than a cog, some species of heir apparent to power, would one day be ground as small as he was. The only question now was when.

And of course he was quite untrained and would stay so. You couldn't properly train the Lissdales since they wouldn't accept the discipline. Crophead sighed softly for he'd made a mistake; he'd put pressure on Lissdale, then refused him clear orders. That was often effective with fully trained men but with a man like Lord Lissdale it was asking for trouble.

For Lissdale had promptly panicked. Fool. To start with he'd hired two outside men, something he'd had no right to do, something to raise the professional's neck hair. Then he'd sent them round to Russell's flat with instructions to beat the diaries from Russell, a plan from a long since amended manual, a ploy to make men like Crophead spit. Double fool. Did he really suppose that a man like Russell, an ex-official who knew what he did, would be left in a flat quite unprotected? Lissdale had tried to make contact since, but Crophead had refused all calls and the messages he had left unanswered. But the man who'd been watching Russell's movements had reported the little he'd managed to see and the story made Crophead sweat in shame. Lissdale's apes had gone in for perhaps seven minues, then a man had arrived in a very fast car and he'd opened Charles Russell's door with a key. Three minutes later a posse of police, and the man had gone one way, the police another, taking Lord

Lissdale's hired hoodlums with them. Triple fool. They might not directly implicate Lissdale for it was hard to believe he had hired them in person, but if they did know and grassed, landing Lissdale in jail, then Crophead would go there and dance on the doorstep.

He corrected the thought since it wasn't accurate; he was anxious to settle with Lissdale directly. This outrageously feeble plan apart there'd been a failure at Fenton Omerod's villa. A valuable life had been lost for nothing, a life worth a dozen Lord Lissdales and more. Lord Lissdale would have to pay for that and Crophead would happily take the payment. That side could wait and be dealt with at leisure, but meanwhile the diaries were hopelessly compromised, or rather the chances of getting them were. Their keeper had been put on notice and their keeper had solid power behind him.

Crophead began to think hard and clearly and he thought as Charles Russell had said he would. If Russell had the diaries still then Russell was a protected man, but they couldn't be sure he did still have them. True that Russell hadn't been near his bank. So what? There were a dozen ways he could pass out papers and if he'd done so they'd be somewhere secure. Lord Lissdale might think of some mad further action, but to Crophead who played with the odds that was finished.

He wrote a note reluctantly and he sent it to his superior. He wasn't a man to cover up and he knew that if he tried he'd fail. It was better to put it straight and hope. He'd had many successes, was high on the ladder, so he simply wrote that he'd finally failed. The diaries were in safe hands and he couldn't reach them.

He put the diaries from his disciplined mind, turning it to his second problem. His instinct was that it was much more serious, potentially a political shipwreck.

. . . We've had that Ambassador's codes for weeks but if there's been anything really first class they've been sending it by courier. Not that they'd tell that old man much but he's been telling them some curious things. Josef Satra, for instance—he thinks he's gone rotten. He may be right at that, it happens, and the trouble with rotten men is rotten actions.

So it had been worth a quiet surveillance, not a round-the-clock tail but an eye on essentials, and what had emerged, though not decisive, had been significant and even disturbing. Satra's Inspector-General had been doing the rounds of his posts in the West and he'd taken Satra out to dinner. But alone and that wasn't protocol. And Satra had a woman here; there was nothing unusual in that, no doubt, but they were often seen in public together and the rumour was he intended marriage.

Cropread methodically locked up his papers, then he walked along the corridor. There was a Counsellor he trusted there. He didn't trust diplomats easily, but this one was his brother-in-law and in Crophead's huge province family was important still.

The Counsellor listened, then nodded agreement. 'I think that you're right to be worried,' he said.

'Of course it may be nothing at all.'

'It can always be nothing at all—or disaster. Satra isn't our subject technically but he comes from a highly sensitive area, so that makes defection worse if it comes.'

'May I ask how you see it? I'd have thought that the British—'

'I don't think you need to lose sleep about them. They hated the last one as much as we did. We made enough fuss to scare them severely and in any case they didn't want him. The eggheads did but the Establishment didn't. It's not soft in the head yet, the British Establishment.' The Counsellor lit a cigarette. 'I think your real worry is worse than that.'

'I'm not sure I follow you.'

'Then put yourself in British shoes. You've a tradition on one side, common sense on the other. So a defector presents himself and asks for asylum. You've just had a very close shave with another, a negotiation suspended and almost a walk-out. What do you do with this second embarrassment?'

'I tell him to go to hell,' Crophead said.

The Counsellor began to laugh. 'You'd be perfectly right but that isn't diplomacy. Nor British politics either, for that matter. You could land your Minister in very grave trouble —every high-minded ass would gang up on him gleefully.

No, you look for an alternative and as it happens I think there is one.'

'What?'

'You'd sell him to another country, the one which would take him and splash the taking.'

'You're serious?'

'That's what I'd do if I were British.'

Crophead weighed it deliberately. 'That,' he said finally, 'that would be disastrous. Much worse than the English, very much worse.' He looked at the Counsellor and he looked at him as a brother-in-law. 'If that were to happen what would my orders be?'

'I doubt if you'd be here to receive them.'

'As bad as that?'

'Every bit as bad.'

'Then I'm asking you for advice if you'll give it.'

'What advice can I give except the obvious? Prevention is better than cure in six languages.'

'You think I should, well, prepare for prevention?'

'I think you'd be very wise indeed.'

'I'd be backed in any action I took?'

'If I have a say you'll be backed to the hilt.'

Crophead weighed it again against long experience. 'It might mean a breach of the law, even violence.'

'How much law to break and when is for you. I can only tell you how I see it. If this Satra does go where I think they'd direct him you'd be vulnerable personally. Whereas if you contrive to stop it, by means which I'd rather you didn't tell me, you'll be recalled in official disgrace perhaps, but the flags will be out where the flags really matter.'

'Is that how you'd really see it in my place?'

'How else could a good official see it?'

Crophead went thoughtfully back to his room but he didn't have time to think as he'd wished. His assistant had been trying to find him and his assistant's face was long and grim. 'Durnford,' he told him, 'has just rung urgently.'

Durnford was in the Foreign Office, one of several fellow-travellers whom Albert Bull already suspected, but he hadn't yet found the evidence to justify any overt action. The price of the rule of law was always high.

Crophead said incredulously: 'Durnford rang us here directly? He must be insane.'

'What he had to say was very urgent.'

'It's still the grossest breach of his orders.'

'I suggest we consider the discipline later.' The assistant began to talk fast and Crophead listened.'

'I'm going to repeat that back to you.'

'Certainly.'

'Josef Satra has called at the Foreign Office?'

'Yes.'

'He was shown up to Albert Bull directly? A mere Military Attaché is shown to Sir Albert Bull himself?'

'That was the message, I haven't yet checked it.'

'You can forget the check, I'm afraid it may fit. Then he leaves in a taxi and goes back to his flat. We know that part from the tail, I take it?'

'Yes, I've had time to talk to the tail. Fortunately he's in radio contact.'

'And what's happening at Satra's flat?'

'The taxi's outside and waiting still.'

'Is that all?'

'Not quite. The driver's been in and came out with a suitcase.'

'Satra's inside still?'

'He's not in the taxi.'

'Oh my God,' Crophead said. He didn't believe there'd ever been one. He thought for ten seconds then picked up a telephone. He wasn't ringing Lord Lissdale nor anyone like him.

For once Russell left the door to Julia as he climbed in himself on the driver's side; he even cut down his starting drill. 'Where did you say that Satra lived?'

'Northumberland Place.'

'That's Bayswater?'

'Up Queensway, then left—'

'Details later. Do your belt up.'

He began to drive as she'd never seen him. At the top of Whitehall he jumped his first red, slipping left to the Mall against the signal. Past the Palace with something less than respect, racing up Constitution Hill to the quadriga. The tangle at Hyde Park Corner slowed him, but once in the Park he was off again strongly, weaving from lane to lane without shame. At the Arch he was lucky, unchecked to the left, slipping into the Carriage Drive, then out of the Park and across the artery into traffic he knew no way to avoid. For the first time he spoke in the mill of Queensway, forcing his way through the gaps in third. Julia Hartley hadn't spoken either.

'Left at Westbourne Grove, right at Chepstow Road?' He'd lived here once and knew the area.

'The next parallel to that and beyond it. House on the right about half way up.'

At the junction an amber came up against him, then the red as he swung brutally right. There was a blare of horns from the column he'd raped but Russell drove hard across its head. Somebody braked but not Charles Russell.

'Close,' she said coolly.

'Just fairly close.'

In Northumberland Place they saw the taxi. A man was walking down the steps. He had a night bag in one hand, a dispatch case in the other. Russell glanced in his mirror and signalled right but the car behind him hooted a warning. For an instant he hesitated, seeing no point in a crash to end with. The big grey car passed him smoothly and fast, but it didn't pull into the left again. Instead it ran up to just short of the taxi. The front wheels, Russell saw, were left locked for the getaway.

He was climbing out fast but a fraction too late. The man who'd been walking down the steps was opening the taxi's door. Three others jumped out of the big saloon and in ten seconds of disciplined violence they had him. One struck him down and two others lifted him. The door of the grey car slammed as it started.

It left a bag in the gutter, forlorn and broken.

Julia had given a single cry but he knew her too well to suppose she'd panic. The taxi driver ran into the house.

'Sensible,' Russell said. 'He'll phone the police.'

'Don't we go after them?'

133

'Pointless to try. Even if we could stay on their tail there are two of us and neither armed.'

'Yes, I suppose so.' She didn't sound sure of it.

'Anyway I can guess where they're going.'

'You can?' She named an embassy.

'No, I don't think so.' He looked at her in sharp inquiry. 'That *was* Josef Satra?'

'It was indeed.'

He'd never met him, or had he? In ten seconds he'd seen a little, enough. . . . The suit had been very good indeed and Russell could guess within a street who had made it and what the work had cost. And the shoes had matched the suit in excellence. So a man of maybe forty who could afford good clothes and wore them elegantly. Held himself well and easily, head back. Maybe a soldier, maybe not. A man who didn't shoot in the back. Rather a dull man, he'd seemed, but decent.

'What are you going to do?' she was asking.

'I'm going to the Executive. At once.'

'But I though you said—'

For the first time since she'd known him he showed a flash of irritation; he hated to hear himself quoted back especially when it was out of context. 'I know what I said, that we couldn't use them. That was perfectly true but it isn't now. The reason we couldn't use them before was the danger they wouldn't see it as we did. They might have thought of it as they're paid to think, that your father was going to do something to harm us. Now all that's behind us, a masque to pass ten minutes before the play.' He looked at her dourly. 'Your father's unimportant now, the diaries are unimportant, so is his book. We're in a very dangerous world indeed.'

'I'd realized that from what happend at Tuke's. And now. . . .' She broke off on what in another woman might almost have been the edge of tears, then said with a sort of savage composure: 'This horrible world and the men who live there—'

'They've the means to check on any man's movements and perhaps they already suspected what Satra intended.'

'They being those who least love defectors?'

'They being those who won't stand for another, especially when he's from Satra's country, especially an official, a diplomat.'

'You thought very fast at Tuke's,' she said.

'I had to think fast. Not that all this is entirely new ground. After thirty years one does get hunches. The trouble is they had ten minutes' start.'

'And now you're using the Executive?'

'Yes. In the first place, as I rudely told you, your father's unimportant now. Secondly I called them last night and I owe them an explanation of that. And thirdly I've told you something else, something about the Security Executive.'

'I'm sorry if I've forgotten it.'

'I told you that they were counter-punchers and now they've got something to counter-punch. Daylight snatches of foreign diplomats. . . .'

He left it unfinished : she didn't press him. He knew these appalling ropes and she did not. 'I liked Satra very much,' she said.

Russell noticed the tense but he didn't comment. 'Enough to try to help him?' he asked.

'Of course. Of course.'

'Then I'm going to the Executive now but I'll call for you again this evening. The timing will depend on them but be ready at midnight unless I ring.'

'I really could help?'

'I think you might.'

She knew that she risked annoying him but she had to ask the essential question. 'Where are we going?'

'The Essex marshes.'

'What's in the Essex marshes?'

'Marsh.'

She gave it up. 'We're going alone?'

'In one sense,' he said, 'we'll be going alone.'

CHAPTER FIFTEEN

At midnight, driving Julia eastwards, Russell was humming quietly again, not opera this time but what she thought was

Cole Porter. He was a man of catholic musical tastes. He had recovered his urbanity but she knew him too well to ask tiresome questions. She would have liked to know why he'd brought her at all, on this certainly sinister midnight mission with the Executive holding a hand in the play. The answer would have astonished her. Provided she wasn't the type to panic, and Julia Hartley had never been that, a woman was superb insurance, less against violence planned and essential than against the sudden flare of temper in a crisis which was going wrong, the regrettable action which would later be regretted. Charles Russell was properly bored with gunplay; he'd seen enough in a week to last his life-time. He snorted disgustedly. Guns in the back and guns through car windows. And beatings-up. One against Omerod, partly successful, another against himself which had failed. Daylight snatches in quiet London streets. . . . At sixty it was undignified. That nonsense was apt for Fifty-five but it wasn't the way the Executive did things. If his plan worked tonight there would be no violence—there wouldn't, that is, if both sides kept their tempers, and a handsome cool-headed and sensible woman was the best insulation Charles Russell knew against the dangerous spark of the sudden Slav temper. After all, he reflected, they weren't barbarians. They were brutal and often excessively ruthless but punctilious as Spanish Dons when it came to a question of public manners.

What was more she was a journalist.

A handsome cool-headed and sensible woman. . . . Hm. Charles Russell didn't know of it but Julia's editor had once thought the same : if Julia Hartley owned a fault it was really that she was too sensible, too civilized. Charles Russell would not have agreed with that for his catholic tastes weren't confined to music, and since he'd always given as well as received his relations with women had been happier than the editor's. The trouble with sensible women, though, was that a man who looked only at what he saw would think of them as simply, well, sensible. Kendal Hartley, for instance—Charles Russell had met him. He was as clever as any man ought to be and sensitive too in the modern manner but Russell had never thought them a match. That was the word; he wasn't a match; he wasn't a match to Julia Hartley. So if she'd had an affair with Josef Satra that would be perfectly natural and proper. Kendal Hartley was safely abroad and they'd been discreet. Charles Russell would have been much put out if you'd said he had a with-it mind, but a genuine and more deep-rooted tolerance was part of his age and private heritage. He said in his urbanest manner:

'You said you liked Satra very much.' He had noticed the tense though he hadn't then commented.

'I still do.'

'I rather think I like him too.'

'I didn't know that you'd ever met him.' Julia was surprised and showed it.

'I didn't think so either till we saw him in that trouble this evening. But the type was the same, very much the same.'

'The same as what?'

'The same as the man who stuck me up when I was staying at your father's house.'

She thought it over. 'You're sure of that?'

'Of course I'm not sure, he was wearing a mask, but the piece would fit as they often do. He was after the diaries, of course to suppress them. Equally logically the other side tried to get them to use them.'

'I'm sorry if Josef Satra misused you.'

'He didn't and that's the point of it. He could have but he didn't do it. In a sense I've a negative debt to him but I'd like to repay it just the same.'

'That all seems a long time ago,' she said.

'These affairs do develop—that's why they're interesting. Satra's the only link with Act One. Act Two, I'm afraid, is much more dangerous. Generally and especially for Satra. He's defected and that's never acceptable. Not acceptable to a major Power.'

For the second time in a single evening she showed an emotion she normally hid. 'You mean to protect him?' she asked. Her voice was taut.

'Protect him from what? From defection—no. He's committed himself and he can't withdraw, but if everything goes as I hope it will we might prevent his being kidnapped by force. That would leave him with a legitimate choice.'

'Of making another life for himself?'

'If everything goes according to plan.'

'He was a decent man,' she said at last.

He'd privately used the adjective once but from a woman it astonished him. 'A *decent* man?'

'I think it's the word. He doesn't shoot men down nor club them pointlessly. That attack on father genuinely distressed him.' She hesitated but decided to tell him. 'And what he wanted of me was just old-fashioned marriage.'

'Which naturally you didn't consider.'

'How could I consider it? A foreign country, an alien world. And I'll tell you something else about Satra.' She was talking in quick rushes now, using Russell as the confessional, glad it was there. 'In the months I knew him I saw him smile twice.'

'There are worse things than not laughing much.'

'Such as knocking people about for the love of it? You're perfectly right but it doesn't change it. I couldn't last long with a man that serious.'

Russell had slackened speed as she talked but he looked at the dashboard clock and increased it. The road had been poor since they'd left the A13 and now as he turned from the B-road it deteriorated sharply again. The Mercedes bumped and lurched protestingly but Russell pushed it firmly on. There was most of a moon behind broken cloud, and in the breaks it was surprisingly light. The drab salt flats lay sullen and dully colourless, seeming interminable, denying horizon, broken by dykes and clusters of reed, an occasional clump of scrub stark as mourning. These were the bad lands and Julia said so. Her moment of emotion had gone.

'Who on earth lives here?'

'A surprising number of people live here.' He smiled as he answered the townswoman's question. People always contrived to live in places, Brazilian rain forests, the desert of Sind. His own thought had been rather different, not how many people lived here but what did they grow. He'd sometimes travelled this road before but always by night and he couldn't be sure. Sugar beet, he supposed, and with great good fortune a little barley, not malting barley but barley for fodder. But what kept the wolf from the door was the birds, the shooting rights or the shooting directly. These creeks had once been alive with fowl, and though wickedly over-shot today there were still the birds if you knew your business. Charles Russell had long lost the taste for killing, but on nights like this and sometimes brighter a casual prowl had raised mallard and widgeon, pochard and a visiting shoveller, a handful of wily and desperate geese.

'What a place to suggest an airport,' she said.

'But we're quite a long way from that, you know.'

'Where are we then?'

'We're off the map.'

She could see it was true : any road had been long since left behind them. But Russell appeared to know his way. There was a track which he seemed to sense though she couldn't and presently a rusty iron bridge. Russell squeezed the Mercedes across it with caution.

'It was just about safe a year ago, but fine fools we'd look in three feet of foul water.'

'Fine fools and very useless ones.'

'I don't guarantee that we're going to be useful.'

They bumped on for perhaps a mile on a causeway, water sulking on either side in the moonlight. Russell had long since turned off the headlights and he drove on the bund very slowly indeed. Presently the water left them, the causeway reluctantly broadening into land. There was even some ragged cultivation but the smell of the sea was stronger than ever. He turned off the sidelights too and stopped. The car was in the lee of a patch of scrub.

He looked at her shoes and nodded approvingly. 'I did say the Essex marshes.'

'I listened.'

'A paragon amongst women. . . . Now.' He was suddenly entirely businesslike. 'This is a sort of island since there isn't a better word for it.'

'Is this the only way onto it?'

'No. On the other side of that scrub there's a broken-down farm. Also a more or less orthodox road to it.'

'People actually live here?' She sounded horrified.

'They really do.'

'What sort of people?'

'Since you seem to like laughing I'll tell you what people. The farm's owned by a communist painter, a bad one. There are critics who admire his abstracts, though the general opinion is they're daubs. Not that he has to sell the things; he has private means as that type mostly has. In his case rather more private than usual.'

As he'd expected she laughed. 'Won't he hear us here?'

'Once we're through that scrub you must go pretty quietly, but they won't hear us unless you shout.' He had answered with the confidence of a man who'd passed a country boyhood. 'The wind's blowing the other way quite hard.'

'They? Your painter friend has company, then?'

'My painter friend won't be there at all, they turn him out when there's serious business.' He took her hand. 'I'll lead you if you'll let me, please. That scrub is what passes for high ground here, which means it's about five feet above highest tide. That's why we came this way, we've got to *see*. No point in knocking up communist painters if in fact there's nothing happening.'

'And what do you expect to see?'

'I expect to see a helicopter. And go carefully, please, there's a canal to cross still. I know you can't see it, I know it's there. You could walk straight in if you didn't know. That's why it's there, very cleverly sited.'

'I can't see any canal from here.'

'You're not meant to see it, you could simply fall in. On one occasion a snooper did. A messy way to die at that.'

'He drowned?'

'When he was found he was full of water. In that sense you could say he drowned.'

He led her up to the countersunk canal. It was wider than she'd expected to find it and evidently man-made and new. There were wooden steps to a mooring post and a small rubber dinghy which moved lazily on a rising tide.

Charles Russell hesitated. He knew all about the canal which faced them for the Executive had warned him strictly. Every hideout must have a safe escape but that escape must also be safe from intrusion. And this one was very safe indeed. When the boat wasn't there as its owners' insurance the barrier was absolute. The water wasn't kept live but you musn't fall in. Flounder about or try to wade and your feet would catch a tripwire and then. . . .

Then the tide would wash you out in time and there wouldn't be a wound or a scar. You'd be just another stranger drowned. There were several a year; this was treacherous country.

So Russell considered the dinghy uncertainly. It was smaller than they'd warned him it would be and it was clear that they couldn't both use it together. . . . Tell a woman that if she upset she'd die? Even the steadiest, even the Julias, could be forgiven for losing their nerve if you did. He said, his voice casual :

'Get into that dinghy and do it gently. Sit with your back to the bows, facing me. You'll see a rope in the stern and you pull on it steadily. There's a pulley each side and the rope's continuous. That way it works from either bank. I'll get it back for myself when you're safely over.' He looked at her. 'You think you can do it?'

'Kendal played with a boat at weekends and I went with him. I've been in a rubber dinghy before.'

'Don't capsize it,' he said.

'It's too cold for bathing.'

He watched her, trying to hide his tension. In the middle there was a stir of wind, funnelled by four or five feet of bank into something which was almost a gust.

The dinghy rocked dangerously.

'Steady ! Sit still !'

She didn't answer but rode it. When the flurry of wind had passed she pulled steadily on.

He watched her land and retrieved the dinghy. He would have liked a change of underclothes.

When he too was across he stretched instinctively, then they walked to the salt scrub and almost through it. As it thinned on the further side he pulled her down. The moon was clear of cloud, they could see. Charles Russell raised an arm and pointed. 'It's safe to talk still but please talk quietly. That's the farm down there.'

'But it's not so broken-down,' she said. 'It looks like a rich man's weekend hideout.'

'I told you the communist painter had money. The same sort of money Lord Lissdale has.'

'From the way you were talking to Harry Tuke I thought you wanted Lord Lissdale forgotten.'

'I wanted you both to forget him—I haven't. I haven't forgotten Lord Lissdale at all.'

She looked again. 'I can't see a helicopter.'

He handed her his nightglasses. 'To the left of the farm, at ten to twelve. Say three hundred yards beyond it. There used to be a small landing strip too, but nowadays that isn't necessary.'

'I think I see.' She was clearly troubled. 'But surely if it's arrived and they're ready—'

He looked at his watch and shook his head. Timing was going to be very important. Arrive too late and you bought yourself an anticlimax : arrive too early and you lost the essential tool of surprise. They'd have too much time to think it out, perhaps even time for instructions by radio. Russell's plan was one he believed could succeed but there was an element of shock in it. Shock wouldn't stand up to men in offices.

'We've still at least half an hour to wait. No chopper-pilot likes flying by night, especially without ground directions, and this one will keep silence for certain. As it's half-light he'll slip across the Channel and after that it doesn't matter.'

'When's dawn?'

'In an hour. But I need half an hour to do what I mean to.'

'There's half an hour to wait, then?'

'Say twenty-five minutes. It's got to be timed just right or nothing.'

'Can I smoke?'

He nodded but refused one himself. So far she'd been exemplary, as cool as a poacher's wife holding his bag. There was plenty to come though; events could go wrong. Anything unexpected and he didn't have an answer to it. He watched the minutes crawl by interminably.

At last he rose and signalled her up. 'Time to go down to the farm,' he said.

'We're going to walk straight up to it?'

'We are if they let us.' He hesitated again but he had to tell her. 'I'm afraid this is the dangerous bit.'

'Why?'

'Some peasant behind a rifle.'

'I see.'

She saw but she started walking with him. He walked deliberately with his guardsman's stride. Julia Hartley took four to his three.

They were nearing the house when the shot came past them, the unmistakable crack of a bullet. The report of the rifle came a split second later. Russell pulled her down on an instant reflex, falling himself in the some smooth movement. He'd moved impressively fast for a man of sixty.

For a moment she lay in silence and he could hear her breathing quicked than usual. Then she said in a perfectly normal voice :

'They can see us here, there's no sort of cover.'

'That was a warning, they won't fire again.' He was hoping that he was telling the truth. 'Their marksmanship is too good for a miss.'

'I hope you're right.'

'I believe I am.' He had raised his head three inches and could see. A jeep was coming out from the stable, a searchlight sweeping the sour flat ground. It fixed them almost at once and held.

'Don't move.'

'I won't.'

The jeep came up fast, its lamp unwavering. Its tyres tore the sullen soil as it braked. Two armed men got out with bayonets fixed.

'Time to stand up,' Charles Russell said. He put out a hand to help her rise but Julia had risen alone. One of the men moved forward menacingly. He put his bayonet in Russell's ribs.

. . . And now a bayonet, that makes a change. Guns, rubber truncheons, bayonets, the book.

Russell knew a few words of the language and used them; he also used his parade ground voice.

'Take me to your commander at once.'

There was a moment of astonished silence. 'Yes, Comrade General.'

'I'm not a General.'

'Yes, Comrade Colonel.'

'That's better. Move.'

'Get into the car, please.'

'Thank you.'

He handed Julia Hartley in.

In the Security Executive they were talking after Russell had gone. The decision had been taken, the firm commitment as firmly given, but these were practically-minded experienced men and they liked to be sure of the practical details. The man Bull called It would have found himself lost, the atmosphere uncongenial, matter-of-fact.

The three top men were sitting comfortably round a table. Crophead had once allowed the reflection that Russell's successor was not yet in his class, but he was an admirable chairman of any meeting and he knew good advice when he heard it clearly. He was saying now, inviting comment:

'I've never seen Russell so angry before. He wasn't even trying to hide it.'

'He wasn't from us.' It was Number Two speaking. He'd had reasonable hopes of Russell's chair but was known to hold strong political views. Presently they were also unfashionable. Another man might have soured and resigned but this one soldiered on philosophically. 'Certainly he was furious. Two hoodlums burst in and tried to beat him. Not even pros to make it worse.'

'Worse?'

'More insulting.'

'What happened about the police, by the way?'

'Nothing—as Russell said it would. Our duty dog was there when they came and the sergeant knew him for what he was. So one of the head men rang us discreetly and we told him that Russell had used his Line. When the duty dog arrived on the scene there were two obvious bad men in Russell's flat and he told him to call the police, which he did. That was wonderfully true as far as it went so they're charging the pair with some ordinary crime. The head man

144

sounded sceptical but we've always played very strict ball when it's mattered. He'll swallow his doubts like the friend he is.'

There was the easy laugh of men at ease. 'But Russell himself thought Lord Lissdale had hired them.'

'That's what makes him so angry. He loathes the man.'

'You think we should have discounted that? In assessing his idea, I mean?'

'I do not. His own feelings apart, and I'd share them myself, I think his plan is the best that's open. Of course it's not guaranteed but nothing is. And none of us could think of a better.'

'You think they'll accept what he means to offer?'

'In the circumstances it's a fair exchange.'

Number Two lit a pipe as the talk went on. It had always amused him that the popular picture of work in Security should diverge so sensationally from what it was. People thought that those mountebanks in Fifty-five were typical and even praiseworthy. Number Two despised them as clumsy clowns. In the Executive matters were handled differently. To begin with it wasn't a truceless war: at least a third of the time you were actively co-operating. There was a surprising amount of common ground, even an occasion, still gratefully remembered, when the Executive had quietly killed an especially silly scheme of Fifty-five's. And relations at the top were excellent. They were, that is, when the two men concerned weren't mercilessly in dispute on some vital interest. Russell, Number Two remembered, had once been a guest of the Colonel-General's. It seemed that they'd shot a bear together, or rather Charles Russell had taken his camera. The Colonel-General had done the shooting, and very poor sport Charles Russell had thought it. The bear had been half asleep still, a sitter.

So for part of the time there was truce of a sort and even when there was war there was understanding. Never spoken and far less committed to paper, it wasn't the less effective for that. There were things you could do, quite illegal things, and the other side wouldn't make too much fuss. A protest perhaps through the usual channels, an affair for some diplomat's stuffier manner. But once step outside what was quietly tolerated and the understanding was simple and perfectly clear : the other side was entitled to step out too. In nine cases in ten it promptly did so, for prestige was at stake as well as politics.

Kidnappings now—that was wholly typical. There were abductions you turned a discreet blind eye on, some man on a stretcher at London Airport, doped to the eyes, going home for treatment. . . . Yes, but one of their nationals too. You interfered at your risk and at negative profit; you didn't want the man here in any case. But snatching a foreign national publicly, a diplomat too to inflate the enormity, was clearly not an affair for tolerance.

'Charles Russell was perfectly right, I think. We're obliged to react and react pretty fast. If we let them get away with that there's no knowing what they won't think of next. Some politician maybe, perhaps a big one.' Number Two's voice was deceptively casual. 'Suppose they took a fancy to the Prime Minister himself. We couldn't have them snatching at a Prime Minister, now could we?'

'Couldn't we?'

'Well. . . .'

There was a comfortable laugh round the comfortable chairs. Number Two never hid his political views. Charles Russell's successor turned away to the third man.

'You're the operations expert. Tell us.'

'It's not watertight—nothing's watertight. But Russell could very well pull it off.'

'Suppose they're not using that farm after all.'

'Where else would they use? Hardly an airport.'

'A private plane?'

'At five thousand a throw? That's the going rate for a really hot cargo. They've always been rather careful with money, and anyway think of the extra risk. Some out-of-work pilot to talk in his beers—'

'All right, so they'll probably use the farm. That's what it's there for anyway—that and some other odd jobs which aren't relevant. But what about Lord Lissdale afterwards?'

'I shouldn't have thought he'd have been our worry.'

'I meant the publicity.'

'That should break in our favour, all grist to the competent journalist's mill. Once it's known where he's gone all his cover will be useless, even spice to a good newspaper story. . . . See how he played us up, the cunning bastard. . . .'

Russell's successor looked back at his Number Two. 'And he usually dines at his club on Tuesdays?'

'Usually. We told you it wasn't watertight.'

'And you're a member there yourself?'

'I am.'

'The taxi has been warned?'

'It has.'

The chairman looked round the meeting, his glance inquiring. 'Any more comments?'

There were no comments.

CHAPTER SIXTEEN

The room was long with a low-beamed ceiling, comfortably even luxuriously furnished. Crophead rose from his chair as Russell and Julia Hartley came in. 'Colonel Russell,' he said. 'An unexpected pleasure. And the lady?'

'Mrs Kendal Hartley.'

'Sir Fenton Omerod's daughter? Ah.' Unknowingly he threw Julia's words back. 'That affair seems a very long time ago.' His manner was formal but quietly friendly. Lord Lissdale would never have known this man, but Lord Lissdale was a hireling with annoying and quite absurd pretensions whereas Russell you could respect and treat with. 'May I offer a drink?'

'It's a little early.'

'Some coffee then?'

'That's very kind.'

When the coffee came it was black and strong and as Russell sipped it Crophead talked easily. 'That affair has developed and not to our liking. I may say "our" since you're not here for nothing? Sir Fenton's book if he does go on with it, those diaries you snatched by a matter of minutes—all water under the bridge by now. A major defection is much more critical.'

'Or rather the steps which you took to prevent it.'

'Yes, I'd heard there were unexpected witnesses. You thought very fast if you'll let me say so.' Crophead, still courteous, started feeling his way. 'And you knew about this farm,' he said. 'You're very well informed indeed.'

'We've known for months and we don't object. Not to the normal traffic, that is.'

'To the normal traffic?'

'No, why should we?'

The normal traffic was simply gold and almost none of it went to the usual black market. It was sold for a modest sterling premium and some surprising officials had at times been glad to purchase it. Charles Russell concealed an ironical smile. . . . Of course if they'd overplayed their hand, started flooding it in and creating a scandal. . . . But no, they had shown no signs of that, they'd always been extremely discreet. They liked their few pounds of extra sterling and were scrupulous about where they spent it. There were politicians who'd think the arrangement criminal but economists, mostly a little old-fashioned, who'd think first of the laws of supply and demand and consider the matter at worst forgivable. The Executive didn't presume to judge. It knew about Pilate's Farm and it knew its use. It was a classic occasion for classic tolerance, but gold was rather different from people. People, especially when not one's own nationals, were outside any understanding. Well out.

'So you don't object to the *normal* traffic.' The manner had sharpened but not the voice. 'If I may say so that's quite in character.'

'I take that as a compliment.'

Crophead looked hard at Julia, thinking. So this was the woman he'd heard about, but why had Charles Russell brought her here? To plead for a lover? That wasn't Charles Russell.

Who had read his thought at once and answered it. 'Mrs Hartley is a distinguished journalist.'

'I see.' There was a reflective pause while Crophead balanced it; he said at last coolly, stating it as a matter of fact: 'There are times when that profession can be, well, a little dangerous.'

148

'Very true. Naturally it's known where we are, but you've plenty of time to act if you wish to. But I've a modest bet with myself you won't.'

. . . He's got something up his sleeve, he must have.

'It's obvious I can do nothing, er, final, and I wouldn't dare abduct you either. I'll admit that to Colonel Russell freely. But I could put you both out of action and—'

'And what? Short of killing or abduction it would only be a question of time. You'd have Satra away and where you want him and to that extent complete success, but a story tied to your heels for ever. You're more than wise enough to weigh the two. Suspicion is one thing—protests and diplomatic rumpus. But a witnessed story is quite another, especially in the *Sunday Gong*. If one of my people had dropped *that* on my desk I wouldn't have been pleased with him.'

Crophead took it without a blink; he even laughed. Charles Russell had worked for a different world but in it he'd held a unique position, certainly senior to Crophead's in his. And he was playing his cards quite beautifully. A disciplined deference was now real respect.

'You're thinking of my Colonel-General?'

'I didn't mention your Colonel-General.'

'I know you didn't—you're far too adroit. But you know perfectly well I have to consider him. I also know that you once went shooting, a small return, if I have it right, for your valuable co-operation.'

'I did have that honour once.'

'Just so.'

This time there was a longer silence till Crophead said sharply: 'It isn't enough.' He sounded almost reluctant to say it.

'To force your hand? I know it isn't. But I didn't came here to force your hand.'

'*Then why did you come?*' Unexpectedly it was Lissdale's Crophead.

Charles Russell ignored the bark and explained. 'I came to offer a *quid pro quo*.'

'What *quid pro quo*?'

Charles Russell told him: he nodded quietly. 'Let me get

149

this perfectly straight, if I may. I give up Satra but take the other?'

'As I see it you'll have to deal with him anyway. He's blown wide open and therefore dangerous. After that little gaffe of his the man's a time-bomb to any sane master.'

'I hope you don't think I had any knowledge—'

'Of that affair in my flat? Of course I don't. I've too much respect for your proven competence.'

'You're generous. If that story got back to the man you mentioned—'

'It won't get back since we don't want you moved. We're beginning to know your mind a little.'

'You think you're beginning to read my mind? Then tell me how it's working now.'

'But that would be an impertinence.'

Crophead began to laugh again. 'What an actor you are,' he said at last.

'Enough to know another one.'

'So that's the proposition?'

'It is.'

'You're really a remarkable man. You come here unarmed and you bring a woman. I've armed men at call and I cannot use them. You talk in that English voice of yours and in ten minutes you have me across a barrel.'

'I don't see it like that. I came to trade. A matter to our mutual profit.'

'And the whole thing done so smoothly it draws the sting. We've something to learn from men like you. Not that we could produce them, though.' He hesitated. 'A detail remains.'

'I'm listening.'

'Nothing gets into your papers of this?'

'That Lord Lissdale has left us less than voluntarily? Certainly not, we don't want that either.'

Crophead stood up with a formal bow. 'I accept your proposition. It's fair.' If his smile was wry it wasn't resentful. 'Besides, you have me screwed to the floor.'

Charles Russell had been wrong in one thing: Lord Lissdale hadn't been getting stick. On the contrary there'd been an ominous silence. There'd been nothing in his usual drop and from his timed calls only recorded 'No message'. Lord Lissdale who knew what could follow displeasure was a very frightened man indeed.

He went down to his club and dined alone, afterwards glumly drinking two brandies. The coffee room was almost empty, the only other man present a man Lissdale loathed. He didn't know him personally but it was known he had connexions with the Security Executive, and in Lord Lissdale's private demonology that made him some sort of fascist lackey. As Lord Lissdale got up the man lit a cigar, using a box of Vestas to do it, fiddling with the box a moment. He didn't need more than a very weak signal, just an impulse to carry to Ryder Street.

In Ryder Street a taxi-driver was illegally waiting and taking a drag. As a light came up on his dash he stubbed it. He drove evenly into St James's Street, swearing softly to see another taxi.

Lord Lissdale was waving the first taxi down when the man from the coffee-room joined him purposefully.

'My cab, I think, sir.'

Lord Lissdale stared—it was most unusual. To begin with he'd certainly been there first, and members of Lord Lissdale's club seldom if ever disputed taxis. Under very great pressure they sometimes tossed. He said stuffily :

'I don't agree.'

'I'm sorry, I must insist on principle. In any case there's another behind.'

'Then why are you making this stupid fuss?'

'It's just that I like to choose my taxis.'

'Oh very well, if you must be tiresome.'

The fascist lackey took the first cab and Lord Lissdale took the second, grumbling.

'Park Crescent, number ninety-seven.'

Lord Lissdale liked to live well and did. He wouldn't have been useful if he'd been living in a garret. Or that, like other left-wing eminents, was what he always told himself.

The taxi was crossing New Cavendish Street when the light came up again on the dash. The driver pressed a button, counting. There was an almost inaudible hiss—that was all. Lord Lissdale half rose, then fell back on the seat.

The taxi swung sharply right, then left, and in the mews there was another car. Three men got out and one opened the taxi. The other two carried Lord Lissdale away. The first had a sort of aerosol spray and he used it in the taxi meticulously.

'Okay, I've finished.'

'I'm properly clean?'

'You're properly clean.'

'Good night, then.'

'Sleep well.'

The man Bull called It might not have admired it. They'd been quiet and efficient, quite unspectacular. The Executive were counter-punchers and they'd had a target here to counter-punch.

Crophead sat down again, turning from Russell to Julia Hartley. 'We've been neglecting you, which is very bad manners. May I offer you a drink again?'

'I'd like one now.'

He clapped his hands and an armed man brought whisky. 'If you were fearing the other thing I'm delighted to disappoint you. I drink it when I must but never here.' He poured generous even lordly shots. 'Half and half with water?' He raised his glass. 'And now to business.'

'I'm glad you see it as fair exchange.'

'But it has to be correctly timed. You've been making the propositions, Colonel. Be good enough to tie them up.'

Charles Russell produced a map and spread it, quoting a precise map reference. 'We left the car there.'

'Did you indeed? And you crossed in our dinghy?'

'I assure you we crossed with appropriate care.'

'Any accident would have embarrassed me.' Crophead's smile was an unspoken apology, Charles Russell's an immediate acceptance. Crophead held out his hand. 'If you'll give me the key I'll have the car fetched. Then the three of you can leave together on delivery of the consideration.'

'I'll do better than that. You can have him now.'

'You mean he's in that car of yours?'

'Nothing so risky and nothing so crude.' Russell passsed over a slip of paper. 'If you'd arrange to have a call to that number. It's the telephone box in the nearest village, but it's dark still, there won't be a soul about.'

'But the call will be answered by one of your people?'

'A man will lose his job if it's not.'

'I doubt if a man will be losing his job, but I don't want my own men compromised.'

'I'd thought of that myself, of course. Ring that number and fix a time to a minute. When your men arrive my own will have left. There'll be nobody there but a man in the call box. He may be down on the floor or they may have propped him. He'll appear to be drunk but I assure you he won't be.'

Crophead began to laugh uninhibitedly. 'You're a pleasure to do business with.' He turned to give incisive orders, then he picked up the whisky lovingly. 'Just time to kill the bottle comfortably. A bottle between respected colleagues.'

CHAPTER SEVENTEEN

Charles Russell had taken a day in bed, feeling that he had properly earned it, but this morning he'd woken to check his engagements. He had three of them, all made by telephone, and for different reasons all would be interesting. The first was with Tuke and Russell was now keeping it, for once sharing the Minister's formidable tea. Tuke never kept drink in his private office since if you did so other people drank it, whereas if you drank it yourself you got nothing done. Harry Tuke was saying amiably :

'So Satra is going where Bull decided.'

'This afternoon and under escort.'

'You think he'll be happy?'

'I'm an ex-official, you musn't talk about happiness. But I know he had no future otherwise. Bad luck if you look at it one way, good another.'

'A lot of his countrymen would sell their souls for the chance. A fine new life—'

'In an alien country.'

'He's alive and forty. What more do you ask?'

'Personally I don't ask a thing, but then I'm Charles Russell not Josef Satra. He got caught in the wheels and that's never agreeable.'

'He owes it to you that he came out alive. I think he's a very fortunate man.'

'You could look at it that way.'

'Don't you?'

'I don't know.'

'I can guess what you mean—you're not a good communist. Satra was, maybe is still, and that leaves a scar. It'll fade soon enough in a brand new country.' The Minister had dismissed Josef Satra but Russell, who hadn't, saw no point in dissent.

Harry Tuke poured more tea but Charles Russell declined it. 'And talking of communists, good and bad, what's the news of the late Lord Lissdale?'

'He isn't yet technically "late", you know. They'll put him through the hoop no doubt, but I don't think they'll do anything final.'

'Meaning you weren't a party to murder?'

'Meaning no more than I'm not revengeful. I like to square my accounts but I don't ask more.'

'And how will you handle the English end?'

'With any luck it will handle itself. Once it's known where he's gone it's an oft-told tale. With variations of course, since his cover was exceptional. But the fact that he posed as a Tory extremist won't stand up for a minute once he's departed. Most of Fleet Street knows what he really was and when the lid comes off they'll play the steam. I wouldn't mind writing the stories myself. And for a change it won't kick back on the Government; just for once it isn't a man from the Foreign Office. It may even do good in its squalid way since you can guess how most papers are going to run it. . . . The enemy within the gates, Trojan Horses in the Royal Enclosure—'

'You ought to have been a journalist.'

'I know several including Julia Hartley. She won't be handling this one, though.'

'She'll be going with Josef Satra?'

'No.'

'But I thought—'

'You thought wrong.'

The Minister looked at some notes, ticking two. 'And Omerod and his despicable book?'

'There can't be a book without the diaries, or if there were it would just be memoirs, and however absurd the memoirs may be they can't do real harm to the country we're thinking of. Albert Bull will be a happy man.'

For a moment the Minister looked uncertain. 'Mrs Hartley said she could handle it if her father turned nasty and took you to court.'

'You doubted her?'

'She's evidently a determined woman. And you said that the diaries were safe themselves.'

'They're very safe indeed,' Russell said.

'You're not telling me more?'

'You don't need to know.'

Tuke shrugged and ticked a final note. 'So we just sit back quietly with fingers crossed?'

'You should always keep your fingers crossed.'

Charles Russell drove on to his next appointment which was one in a private room at Heathrow. An official from the Executive had been sent ahead to explain the visit and Russell was shown in at once. Josef Satra rose and Russell bowed.

'May I introduce myself? My name's Charles Russell.'

'I've heard it—who hasn't? I'm greatly honoured. I hadn't expected a formal send-off.'

. . . No, he isn't pulling my leg; he means it. Julia was right, this man is *serious*. He'll do marvellously where he's going now.

'I'm afraid that it isn't formal at all. I just came to say that I hope you'll be happy.'

'That's really very kind of you.' Satra was very stiff indeed.

'No, not kind. We've met before.'

'I don't recollect it.'

'Or perhaps you're too cautious to say you do. I'm the man you held up at Sir Fenton's house, but also you didn't shoot me or club me when either would have been easy to do.'

Unsmiling still Josef Satra considered it. 'Suppose I admitted it, what would you do? Would you stop me and try to lay some charge?'

'Do you want to be stopped?'

'Not now—I'm committed.'

'Unwillingly?'

'I don't know yet.'

'Then I came to wish you a pleasant voyage. I hope you'll be happy, I think you may be.'

'How can I be happy? I've lost all round.'

'Will you suffer an older man to speak? You've lost something which men have lost before and most of them have somehow survived. If that sounds a little cynical it's also one of the facts of life. As for your political background, environment is immensely powerful. If that sounds cynical too I'm sorry.'

'Since it's happened this way I must hope you're right.'

'Then I wish you very well indeed.' Russell held out his hand. 'May I offer a parting word of advice?'

'I'm sure it will be very sound.'

'Never carry a gun if you don't mean to use it. Not even in the United States.'

Russell drove back to his flat and a drink, and at six o'clock started changing leisurely. He had a dinner engagement with Julia Hartley and unfinished business he wished to dispatch. She started talking before he'd let go of her chair.

'I've been spending the afternoon with Bull, and Satra's Ambassador had just been round to talk to him. He started on some extraordinary spiel about Satra's defection and father's book. One paid for the other, he seemed to think, for its suppression Bull thought the old man meant, and Bull, who thinks fast, agreed at once. He could since he knew you had the diaries, and he'd heard through Tuke what I mean to do if father turns nasty and takes us to court. The Ambassador thanked him warmly and left; he said that he'd done his job and was ready to die.'

'*Realpolitik*. Bull would understand that.'

'He understood it very well, but there's more to Bull than simply power-plays. He's got father where he wants him now but he'll also be magnanimous.'

'How?'

'Father had a secret ambition, typically father but not quite ignoble. He wanted to be a magistrate.' She laughed, but unmaliciously. 'To round the picture off, you know—Sir Fenton Omerod, county magistrate.'

'And alas they wouldn't look at him?'

'Do you blame them?'

'Well. . . .'

'Bull says he can fix it when father leaves hospital.'

'God help the locals.'

'They can always appeal.' She was suddenly serious, putting her wine down. 'Tomorrow,' she said, 'I'll be eating with Kendal.'

'Fortunate Kendal.'

'I hope he thinks so. You said once I was a marvellous daughter but I had to be good at something, you see. Something human if only dutiful.'

'The grimmest of human relationships.'

'Yes. Now I'm trying to make another one.'

'Fortunate Kendal,' he said again.

'I can only hope he thinks so too. But there's something to start on : he makes me laugh. The impossible man can make me laugh and I think that's a start for a civilized life.'

'It's very important indeed,' Russell said.

She drank some more wine; she was almost shy. 'Which leaves just one loose end.'

'What's that?'

'The diaries.'

'They're perfectly safe.'

'That's what you said to Tuke. I'm not Tuke. Are they in your bank?'

'They are not.'

'In a safe deposit?'

'Not in a safe deposit.'

'Come clean, Charles, I'll wear it.'

'I burnt them,' he said. 'I felt I had to.'

For a moment she didn't answer him, then she picked up her glass and touched his own. 'You're a very good man, a strange sort of saint.'

'Come off it,' he said, 'before *I* start laughing.'

A SELECTION OF FINE READING
AVAILABLE IN CORGI BOOKS

Novels

☐	552 08651 7	THE HAND-REARED BOY	*Brian W. Aldiss* 25p
☐	552 07938 3	THE NAKED LUNCH	*William Burroughs* 37½p
☐	552 08849 8	THE GLASS VIRGIN	*Catherine Cookson* 40
☐	552 08980 X	THE NICE BLOKE	*Catherine Cookson* 30p
☐	552 08963 X	CAPE OF STORMS	*John Gordon Davis* 40p
☐	552 08981 8	THE SPRING MADNESS OF MR SERMON	
			R. F. Delderfield 35p
☐	552 08966 4	MY FRIENDS THE HUNGRY GENERATION	*Jane Duncan* 30p
☐	552 08934 6	THE INTERNS	*Richard Frede* 35p
☐	552 08912 5	SUCH GOOD FRIENDS	*Lois Gould* 40p
☐	552 08985 0	THE WELL OF LONELINESS	*Radclyffe Hall* 50p
☐	552 08982 6	CLOVIS	*Walter Harris* 30p
☐	552 08125 6	CATCH-22	*Joseph Heller* 35p
☐	552 08984 2	THE CHARTER CHICKS	*Jan Kendrick* 25p
☐	552 08932 X	ALSO THE HILLS	*Frances Parkinson Keyes* 45p
☐	552 08888 X	REQUIEM FOR IDOLS	*Norah Lofts* 25p
☐	552 08949 4	THE MAN FROM O.R.G.Y.	*Ted Mark* 30p
☐	552 08951 6	THE REAL GONE GIRLS	*Ted Mark* 30p
☐	552 08791 2	HAWAII	*James A. Michener* 75p
☐	552 08124 8	LOLITA	*Vladimir Nabokov* 35p
☐	552 07954 5	RUN FOR THE TREES	*James S. Rand* 35p
☐	552 08887 0	VIVA RAMIREZ!	*James S. Rand* 40p
☐	552 08930 3	STORY OF O	*Pauline Reage* 50p
☐	552 08976 1	OUR GANG	*Philip Roth* 35p
☐	552 08597 9	PORTNOY'S COMPLAINT	*Philip Roth* 40p
☐	552 08945 1	THE HONEY BADGER	*Robert Ruark* 55p
☐	552 08372 0	LAST EXIT TO BROOKLYN	*Hubert Selby Jr.* 50p
☐	552 08931 1	ZARA	*Joyce Stranger* 30p
☐	552 07807 7	VALLEY OF THE DOLLS	*Jacqueline Susann* 40p
☐	552 08523 5	THE LOVE MACHINE	*Jacqueline Susann* 40p
☐	552 08091 8	TOPAZ	*Leon Uris* 40p
☐	552 08384 4	EXODUS	*Leon Uris* 40p
☐	552 08866 8	QB VII	*Leon Uris* 50p
☐	552 08983 4	THE TUDOR ROSE	*Julia Watson* 25p
☐	552 08962 1	THE HELPERS	*Stanley Winchester* 40p
☐	552 08481 6	FOREVER AMBER Vol. 1	*Kathleen Winsor* 35p
☐	552 08482 4	FOREVER AMBER Vol. 2	*Kathleen Winsor* 35p

War

☐	552 08952 4	THE PATROL	*Laurie Andrews* 25p
☐	552 08935 4	ACCIDENTAL AGENT (illustrated)	*John Goldsmith* 35p
☐	552 08920 6	SECURITY RISK	*Gilbert Hackforth-Jones* 25p
☐	552 08749 4	SS GENERAL	*Sven Hassel* 35p
☐	552 08779 3	ASSIGNMENT: GESTAPO	*Sven Hassel* 35p
☐	552 08855 2	THE WILLING FLESH	*Willi Heinrich* 35p
☐	552 08986 9	DUEL OF EAGLES (illustrated)	*Peter Townsend* 50p
☐	552 08892 7	THE FORTRESS	*Raleigh Trevelyan* 30p
☐	552 08936 2	JOHNNY GOT HIS GUN	*Dalton Trumbo* 30p
☐	552 08987 7	MASSACRE AT MALMEDY (illustrated)	*Charles Whiting* 40p
☐	552 08919 2	JOHNNY PURPLE	*John Wyllie* 25p

Romance

☐	552 08973 7	MY SISTERS AND ME	*Barbara Perkins* 25p
☐	552 08956 7	MAIDEN VOYAGE	*Alex Stuart* 25p
☐	552 08991 5	RESEARCH FELLOW	*Alex Stuart* 25p
☐	552 08955 9	THE SUMMER'S FLOWER	*Alex Stuart* 25p

Science Fiction

☐	552 08925 7	THE BEST FROM NEW WRITINGS IN S.F. ed.	*John Carnell* 25p
☐	552 08942 7	A WILDERNESS OF STARS	ed. *William Nolan* 30p
☐	552 08804 8	THE AGE OF THE PUSSYFOOT	*Frederik Pohl* 25p
☐	552 08860 9	VENUS PLUS X	*Theodore Sturgeon* 25p

General

☐ 552 08944 3   **BILLY CASPER'S 'MY MILLION-DOLLAR SHOTS'**
       Billy Casper 50p
☐ 552 08768 8   **SEX MANNERS FOR OLDER TEENAGERS** (illustrated)
       Robert Chartham 30p
☐ 552 08926 5   **S IS FOR SEX**   *Robert Chartham* 50p
☐ 552 98958 4   **THE ISLAND RACE Vol. 1** *Winston S. Churchill* 125p
☐ 552 98959 2   **THE ISLAND RACE Vol. 2** *Winston S. Churchill* 125p
☐ 552 98572 4   **NEE DE LA VAGUE** (illustrated) *Lucien Clergue* 105p
☐ 552 08800 5   **CHARIOTS OF THE GODS?** (illustrated) *Erich von Daniken* 35p
☐ 552 08861 7   **THE AUTOBIOGRAPHY OF A SUPER TRAMP**
       W. H. Davies 40p
☐ 552 07400 4   **MY LIFE AND LOVES**   *Frank Harris* 65p
☐ 552 98748 4   **MAKING LOVE** (Photographs) *Walter Hartford* 85p
☐ 552 08362 3   **A DOCTOR SPEAKS ON SEXUAL EXPRESSION**
    IN MARRIAGE (illustrated) *Donald W. Hastings, M.D.* 50p
☐ 552 08992 3   **MASTERING WITCHCRAFT** *Paul Huson* 35p
☐ 552 98862 6   **INVESTING IN GEORGIAN GLASS** (illustrated)
       Ward Lloyd 125p
☐ 552 08069 1   **THE OTHER VICTORIANS** *Steven Marcus* 50p
☐ 553 08664 9   **THE HUMAN ZOO**   *Desmond Morris* 35p
☐ 552 08927 3   **IS DEATH THE END**   *P. & S. Phillips* 35p
☐ 552 08880 3   **THE THIRTEENTH CANDLE** *T. Lobsang Rampa* 35p
☐ 552 08975 3   **THE YOUNG BRITISH POETS** *ed. Jeremy Robson* 30p
☐ 552 08974 5   **BRUCE TEGNER METHOD OF SELF DEFENCE**
       Bruce Tegner 40p
☐ 552 98479 5   **MADEMOISELLE 1 + 1** (illustrated)
    Marcel Veronese and Jean-Claude Peretz 105p
☐ 552 08928 1   **TELL ME, DOCTOR** *Dr. Michael Winstanley* 35p

Western

☐ 552 08907 9   **SUDDEN: TROUBLESHOOTER** *Frederick H. Christian* 25p
☐ 552 08971 0   **TO ARMS! TO ARMS IN DIXIE No. 68** *J. T. Edson* 25p
☐ 552 08972 9   **THE SOUTH WILL RISE AGAIN No. 69** *J. T. Edson* 25p
☐ 552 08131 0   **THE BLOODY BORDER No. 35** *J. T. Edson* 25p
☐ 552 07898 0   **GUNS IN THE NIGHT NO. 15** *J. T. Edson* 25p
☐ 552 08979 6   **THE COWBOYS** *William Dale Jennings* 30p
☐ 552 08995 8   **CATLOW**   *Louis L'Amour* 25p
☐ 552 09027 1   **SACKETT**   *Louis L'Amour* 25p
☐ 552 08939 7   **TUCKER**   *Louis L'Amour* 25p
☐ 552 08922 2   **LAW OF THE JUNGLE No. 13** *Louis Masterson* 25p
☐ 552 08906 0   **SUDDEN: MARSHAL OF LAWLESS** *Oliver Strange* 25p

Crime

☐ 552 08970 2   **KILL THE TOFF**   *John Creasey* 25p
☐ 552 08968 0   **ACCUSE THE TOFF**   *John Creasey* 25p
☐ 552 08977 X   **UNDERSTRIKE**   *John Gardner* 25p
☐ 552 08988 5   **THE HARDLINERS** *William Haggard* 25p
☐ 552 08640 1   **RED FILE FOR CALLAN** *James Mitchell* 25p
☐ 552 08839 0   **TOUCHFEATHER TOO** *Jimmy Sangster* 25p
☐ 552 08894 3   **DUCA AND THE MILAN MURDERS** *Giorgio Scerbanenco* 30p
☐ 552 08884 6   **MY GUN IS QUICK** *Mickey Spillane* 25p

All these books are available at your bookshop or newsagent: or can be ordered direct from the publisher. Just tick the titles you want and fill in the form below.

....

CORGI BOOKS, Cash Sales Department, P.O. Box 11, Falmouth, Cornwall.
Please send cheque or postal order. No currency, and allow 6p per book to cover the cost of postage and packing in the U.K., and overseas.

NAME ....

ADDRESS ....

(JUNE 72) ....